Books by Natalie Babbitt

Herbert Rowbarge

Herbert
Rowbarge

by Natalie Babbitt

Farrar · Straus · Giroux

NEW YORK

Herbert Rowbarge

Foreword

The job of the biographer is not a simple one. Life being what it is—for the most part, crushingly dull —it is often necessary, when writing down a history, to collapse large parts of it like a concertina, compressing its multitude of monotones into a single blat. In reality, it can be stretched out to a great length, like anyone else's history, since every day of it, no matter how tuneless, has been a whole twenty-four hours through which the subject has had to plod. Still, what else is the biographer to do? The life of Herbert Rowbarge, like the topography of Ohio, had a number of interesting crescendos, but the flat parts were more numerous by far.

The biographer will take pains on the following pages to present the crescendos in full, but will leave the flat parts out. Why not? A travelogue writer would do this without a blush. A travelogue writer, describing a motor trip from Cincinnati up to Cleveland, would not shrivel the reader's brain with lengthy descriptions of Xenia or Marion, and might not even pause overlong at Columbus. He would, instead, lean heavily on water for interest. Rivers. Streams. And lakes. Ohio has lots of water.

Herbert Rowbarge was closely associated with water. He was born on the banks of the big river, the beautiful Ohio, and stayed nearby for his first long twenty-two years. And it was one of the lesser lakes, Red Man Lake, that gave back daily reflections of him and the flowering of his ambition through all the years that followed.

Ambition. There's plenty of that in Ohio. Unlikely though it seems, one-fifth of all our American Presidents to date were born in Ohio. No one has any clear idea why. It is a disproportionate percentage, when you consider that the great majority of states have fathered no Presidents at all. Of Ohio's seven, two, it is true, were shot, accounting for exactly one half of our assassinations, and this is yet another disproportionate percentage; but probably there is nothing suspicious about it.

Herbert Rowbarge was ambitious. Still, ambition by itself is not enough. Consider the maple seed. Though it is a hardy little fellow, linked to a twin by a tight outer coat and sharing a pair of "wings," and though it comes equipped with a fixed ambition to establish itself in the world as a handsome and useful tree, it cannot even sprout if it spirals down from its parent to some hostile place: a gutter, a rock, a running brook. In the hurly-burly of wind and wintering, it will almost certainly be separated from its twin and left all alone. If, in the springtime, Nature should somehow favor it with sprouting, it may well be throttled soon after by the wrong amount of rain, while at other times crowding and shadow have been known to do it in. Pine mice lie in wait for it, and it must ever be wary of the dreaded bagworm and the aphid. Finally, it may survive all these only to be uprooted by a passing mole or felled by the horrors of root rot.

Full flower is hard to achieve, then, even in Ohio. Yet Herbert Rowbarge thrived. When, eventually, the Grim Reaper axed him down, it was possible to say of him, as it is of a healthy maple, that he had done in life the very thing he started out to do. And if the end for him was in a heavy mahogany box with silver fittings rather than a sawmill, even so it's the same thing when you come right down to it.

Nevertheless, though he thrived, though he achieved his ends, Herbert Rowbarge was less lucky than a maple tree. A vital piece of him was wrenched away in his third month of life, and in spite of his success in the eyes of the world—indeed, his success in his own eyes—he never recovered from the separation as a maple seed seems to do. He was, in a curious way, only half a person. Love in abundance was given him three times in his life: by his only friend, Dick Festeen; by his wife, Ruby; and by his twin daughters, Babe and Louisa. To none of these did he give his own love back. He couldn't.

He gave nothing back to Ohio, either, though he

took a great deal from it. Still, perhaps it is premature to say that he gave nothing back to Ohio. Whether he did or not depends on the stoutness of that heavy mahogany box with the silver fittings. Certainly it was not his intention to give anything back. But the water and the earth are persistent. They have their little ways. Probably, in time, the debt will be paid.

Tuesday, May 20, 1952

Much has been made of the fact that there have never, in ten times ten thousand winters, been two snowflakes exactly alike. This is considered one of Nature's miracles, and even so much as a single identical pair discovered in even so remote and therefore pointless a place as Igloolik or Murmansk would ruin the whole thing. Yet here, in northwestern Ohio, for everyone with half an eye to see, are Babe and Louisa Rowbarge, sitting face to face at a table in the President McKinley Tea Room, and they are exactly alike down to the last tooth and zipper, and nothing at all is ruined thereby.

And yet there is a marvel here, if not a miracle. All that can be seen with half an eye is two figures dressed alike, plainly unwed, unbedded, undiscovered at nearly forty-five, plumped on the tea room's little chairs like pillows on a sofa. Too much physical ease, too many buttered rolls, have feathered them into a soft and boneless-looking middle age: in height neither short nor tall, their hips wide, their shoulders round, their carton-colored hair sheared and seared monthly into rigid curls around the corner at Miriam's House of Beauty. They are so dime-a-dozen that, instead of exclaiming on their twinship, it seems more logical to wonder idly where the other ten might be—still in the box, perhaps, under a counter, not yet priced and ready for display.

So that's not the marvel, what's available to half an eye. The marvel takes more study and, after a period, will begin to reveal itself: their faces, their expressions, are different from other people's. Elsewhere—in the tea room, outside in Mussel Point, abroad in the go-to-hell world—are faces young and old, wrinkled up or stretched or drooping with the effort to be understood, and loved in spite of it. Not so with the faces of these two. Their eyes are calm as puddles, their cheeks and foreheads are smooth. For no matter what one of them does or says, the other always knows the reason and approves.

Nobody else cares a fig about them—not their father, Herbert Rowbarge; not their dead mother's sister, Aunt Opal Loose; not Walter Loose, their cousin—and this is sometimes a misery, but not as bad as it might have been otherwise.

There's more, not a marvel, maybe, but almost as potent: their father is the owner and creator of the Rowbarge Pleasure Dome. This is not to be sneezed at, and the waitress at the President McKinley Tea Room knows it. She has given them extra butter for their muffins and made quite sure the knives to spread it with are free of flotsam. For without Herbert Rowbarge, there would be no Pleasure Dome, no crowds in the summers, no tea room, nothing—just an untouched, quiet lake the way it was before, and Mussel Point a town of no importance. There would also, of course, be no Babe and Louisa.

Babe stirs sugar into her tea and says, "How's Daddy today?"

"Well," says Louisa, "it seemed to me this morning he was acting kind of funny."

"Funny how?"

"That's just it," says Louisa. "I've been thinking about it and I can't quite put my finger on it."

They do not live together any more, haven't lived together for the last five years. One stays at home with their father and sees to his needs, while the other stays with Aunt Opal and sees to hers. And on the first of every month they change places. Living apart is terrible for them, but everyone else is delighted, especially their father, Herbert Rowbarge.

"He was all right in April," says Babe.

"Most of this month, too," says Louisa, "but this morning he was—I don't know. Like I say, I just can't put my finger on it."

"You worry about him too much," says Babe, patting her sister's hand.

"I suppose so," says Louisa. They smile at each other, and for a while they sip their tea in silence.

Outside—beyond the tea room's concrete path laid out between two truck tires painted white and planted neatly to petunias—beyond the sidewalk—across the quiet road—the public gates to the Rowbarge Pleasure Dome are shut and locked. But the work gate far around the fence is open and the bustle inside is intense. Brooms scratch the back of the boardwalk end to end. Paint, like an ointment, soothes away a winter's worth of parching. Fresh oil and grease are lavished on cams, gears, axles, levers—everything that moves; and everything does move at the Rowbarge Pleasure Dome. It is the best small amusement park in the state, and always getting better: at the farthest end a new ride, a Tunnel of Love, is in its final stages and will open with the park on Memorial Day, just ten days off.

While Babe and Louisa have their tea, their cousin and Aunt Opal's son, Walter Loose, who is manager of the park and someday to be owner, is busy overseeing the installment of ten little swan boats which will cruise the twisting dark of the Tunnel of Love past dim-lit dioramas where cupids, pink and chubby, lean down—hang down, on wires—from wooden moons to draw their bows; neutered babies all, with gauze around their groins. For as such things go, or could go, this ride is rather tame. The little boats will trace their route a short four yards apart, eliminating privacy. And the tour will only take five minutes—too short a time for serious arousal of the blood. Still, it is titillating in its way, and Walter likes it. Walter is forty-two and, like his cousins, unmarried, but, unlike them, no virgin. If it weren't for the fact that he is son to his now-dead father,

Dr. Stuart Loose, and nephew to his uncle, Herbert Rowbarge—in other words, if Walter weren't as rich as he is and due to get richer—the town would long ago have written him off for a wolf, and worse. But things being what they are, he is instead admired and indulged, especially by his mother and the waitress at the President McKinley Tea Room.

"Everything all right?" says the waitress to Babe and Louisa.

"Oh, yes," they say. "Just lovely."

"Anyway, Babe," says Louisa, "we'd better get cracking on some birthday plans. It's only three weeks off."

"I know," says Babe. "Poor Daddy. He always hates his birthdays."

"But if we didn't do something, don't you think he'd be hurt?"

"Well, yes, I do think so, probably. But let's do something different this year. A surprise party, maybe. You know—get everyone together and have a nice dinner at the Inn."

"But, Babe," Louisa reminds her, "the park'll be open by then and the Inn'll be jammed."

"Oh, shoot," says Babe, "I forgot about that. Well, maybe Aunt Opal could do it."

"That would be better, if you can talk her into it. But whatever we do, it ought to be simple, and quiet, I think. I really am kind of worried about him."

Babe looks skeptical. "It doesn't sound to me as if you've got much reason," she says.

Louisa dampens a fingertip and thoughtfully attempts to capture the final crumbs from the napkin flopped open in the muffin basket. "It's just—well, for one thing, he was so *crabby* this morning," she says at last.

"He's always crabby," says Babe.

"Yes, but he seemed really tired, too. I mean, all pale and exhausted. And then he kept squinting with one eye."

"Well," says Babe, "it's probably nothing. After all, he's not a young man any more. Did he go down to the park?"

"Of course. He was there all morning. And he brought Walter back for lunch so they could talk business. I wish he'd slow down, really retire. But he won't."

"Not till he drops," says Babe.

Louisa peers into her cup, sees a last sweet bead of tea, and tips it to her lips. But the bead—like Herbert Rowbarge, perhaps—is too stubborn to let go. It clings to the bottom, bulging, and refuses to slide. She gives up the effort with a sigh and returns the cup to its saucer. "Poor Daddy," she says. "He's always been so alone."

"Nonsense," says Babe. "He's always had us."

"No, but you know what I mean," says Louisa.

They talk about it often, their father's parents' death in a train wreck, his adoption by a wealthy Cincinnati aunt, *her* death and his inheriting all her money, all this long before they were born. They never can decide whether it's a sad story or a lucky one. It doesn't occur to them that it might be neither of these but, rather, a genuine *story*—a tissue, a passel, a whole wide tapestry of lies.

The waitress says, "Can I get you ladies anything else?"

Louisa shakes her head. "We're fine," she says.

They lie, themselves, a little, from time to time.

June 1880

The beginning for Herbert Rowbarge was unusual compared to that of most of us. The process itself was no different, of course; we are told that a substance called oxytocin, manufactured in the pituitary gland, is nearly always responsible for that, bringing on as it does the uterine contractions commonly known as labor, and there is nothing unusual about a pituitary secretion. But there were other features to Herbert's birth which, when viewed from a kindly distance, did give it a suggestion of novelty.

To start with, the blessed event took place in a moldy room upstairs over a riverside saloon, a little after midnight, so that his mother's groans, his very birth cry, were drowned out by the noise of high living from the floor below. The thin, resentful piping of Herbert Rowbarge, newest addition to the human race, was no match for the roar of the world which received him. His arrival went unnoticed except by the immediate participants.

In the second place, the mother of Herbert Rowbarge, a woman of thirty-five with wide hips and a narrow view of the blessings of maternity, was scarcely affected at all by his emergence. Her overriding emotion was one of relief, as one might be relieved by the lancing of a boil. "Thank God that's over," she said when the thing was accomplished. "I'll be up and outa here in no time." At this, the midwife presiding at the birth, a certain Mrs. Mink, pursed her lips but held her peace. Mrs. Mink was a large, suspicious woman with chapped and pendulous upper arms, the legal wife of the saloonkeeper presiding on the floor below. Whereas the mother of Herbert Rowbarge was the legal wife of no one at all, nor did she wish to be. What she did wish to be was off on the next train down along the river to Cincinnati.

In the third place, Herbert Rowbarge was not the only baby to be born at that hour in that place. He had been preceded into the open air by another infant, a brother, whose luminous purple complexion and general appearance of decay he matched in every particular. For nine long months they had swayed together, cheek by jowl, sharing their tight, wet void in perfect if soundless harmony. Now that it was over, they lay again, cheek by jowl, wrapped in blankets and looking anything but new—Herbert the younger by five minutes, but both of them looking old—old and feeble and peevish. They were exactly alike. They were, to speak plainly, identical twins.

The mother of these two rose up on one elbow and looked at them. Mrs. Mink, rolling down her sleeves, looked at them also. "I'll be damned," said the mother at last. Somewhere deep among the buried inner pleatings of her brain, a sense of wonder tried vaguely for the surface, failed, and sank back into limbo. Thus spared from reflection, the mother lay down again and stroked her flattened belly happily.

"What you gonna call 'em?" asked Mrs. Mink.

"Well, lemme see now," said the mother, real interest roused for the first time. "I met a coupla fellas once when I was working the dance halls down to Louisville. I had a little pile saved from my—uh—earnings, so's I could head out for New Orleans, but them two yeggs sweet-talked me into giving every cent of it to them. They was gonna invest it for me in a gold mine. A gold mine! Can you beat that? God, I was dumb in them days. Anyways, they slipped out and left me flat, just like these two. So let's call 'em Herbert and Otto, same as them first two hooligans." She giggled, yawned, closed her eyes, and went instantly to sleep.

Mrs. Mink stretched her mouth into a thin line of disapproval and shook her head. Then she took away the lamp and returned to her duties at the bar.

At dawn, the wailing of the babies brought her again to the birth room, full of instructions for a first feeding. But the mother had taken her milk and vanished, picked up and gone forever without so much as tidying the bed that had cushioned her labor.

In this way was Herbert Rowbarge, and his brother Otto, left alone in the wide, uncaring world. The place was Gaitsburg, on the southeastern edge of Ohio. The year was 1880. The day was June 11, under—what else?—the sign of Gemini.

Mrs. Mink never for a moment considered the possibility that she might keep Herbert and Otto and raise them as her own. It was not so much that she believed there was bad blood in their tiny veins— though of course she did believe it—as it was the fact that Mrs. Mink, though conscientious, was not at all softhearted. She had brought other babies into the world under the same conditions and, except for there being twins this time around, it was an old story and the ending never varied. She merely put on her hat, gathered up the luckless pair, climbed into her buggy, and drove a mile out of town to the Gaits County Children's Home.

It was a golden morning, but Mrs. Mink ignored this feature, and so did Herbert and Otto. The latter were preoccupied with hunger, the former with duty, and none of the three was inclined to be distracted. Arriving at the foot of the hill where the Home stood, Mrs. Mink did not pause to look up and admire the sunstruck windows or the slate roof basking in the warmth. She did not pause to remember that it was the handsomest Home in the state, or to grieve

for the shabbiness, inside, of furnishings and in-
mates alike. Instead, she urged her horse firmly up
the driveway, reined in at the wide veranda, and,
grasping an angry red infant under each arm,
marched up the steps to the door. Here, having no
hand free to ring the bell, she kicked vigorously at
a lower panel with one large, booted foot until at
last the door was opened.

A child of eleven, a girl, in a much-mended dress
and bare feet, was doing service as butler and downstairs maid that morning. She clutched a feather
duster in one grubby hand, and when she saw Herbert and Otto, an expression of deep annoyance
crossed her face. She shook the duster and said,
emphatically, "Goddamn it!"

"Never mind," said Mrs. Mink. "Where's Matron?"

"She's in her office," said the child, pointing reluctantly. "In there."

Mrs. Mink knew the office well from previous
visits. She strode up to its door and, again, having
no hand free to knock, kicked, while the girl stood
by, scowling at Herbert and Otto.

After a moment the door opened and the matron
of the Children's Home emerged.

"Morning, Mrs. Frate," said Mrs. Mink. "Here's
two more."

Mrs. Frate was a thin, kindly woman of fifty, pale
with the pallor of one who yearns only for peace in
this world but, knowing she is unlikely to get any,
struggles to be grateful without it. When she saw

Herbert and Otto, the struggle intensified. Her face went even paler and she gasped, "Oh, no, Mrs. Mink! We can't!"

"You got to," said Mrs. Mink.

"But we have too many already! And Cook will raise the roof! All that milk to warm and food to mash . . ."

"Cook'll manage," said Mrs. Mink. "You don't expect *me* to keep 'em, do you? Here, take 'em. I got to get back—I got work to do."

The girl standing by said, again, "Goddamn it!"

"Hush, Clarissa," said Mrs. Frate. She received the babies into her own arms, shaking her head resignedly, and asked, "Do they have names?"

"Herbert and Otto," said Mrs. Mink.

"Which is which?"

"It don't matter," said Mrs. Mink. "You can't tell 'em apart anyways. Ugly, ain't they?"

At this point the babies, now seriously hungry, began to wail again, waving purple fists helplessly and exposing wide stretches of gum. Mrs. Mink, raising her voice over the racket, said, "Well, I got to get back." And with a flurry of relief, she disappeared.

Clarissa banged the big front door shut behind her and once more brandished the duster. "We gonna have to take care of 'em?" she demanded.

"It looks that way," said Mrs. Frate. She straightened her shoulders, adjusting the double burden. "It's our duty, Clarissa."

"Goddamn it!" said Clarissa.

One morning in early September, a wagon arrived at the Children's Home, and soon, in Mrs. Frate's sitting room, Herbert and Otto were displayed to Mr. and Mrs. Emil Schwimmbeck, a solemn young farmer and his eager wife.

"This all you got?" said the farmer severely. "They look kinda puny to me."

"Oh, no, Emil!" said his wife. "They're sweet! What are their names?"

"Herbert and Otto," said Mrs. Frate. She laid the pair down side by side on the sofa, where they peered upward vaguely, folding and unfolding fists which were no longer purple but had turned quite pink and normal. They were quiet now, having just been fed by the still-indignant Clarissa. "They're three months old," said Mrs. Frate, with thinly veiled hope, "and very strong and healthy."

"Here's the way it is," said Emil Schwimmbeck. "We're headed north, up near Sandusky. Got some land waiting. I need a good boy to help with the work and I'd sure rather have a growed one than something like this. Thing is"—he lowered his voice—"we just lost a baby of our own and Doc says we'd better not try again, but Mabel here's still got her heart set on a little one, so . . ."

"I understand," said Mrs. Frate. "It's only natural."

"Which is which?" asked Mabel. She had knelt on the floor before the sofa and was offering a finger to each baby.

"The one with the ribbon on his wrist is Otto," said

Mrs. Frate. "We put it there so we could tell them apart. They're so very much alike otherwise."

"Oh, Emil, couldn't we take them both?" said the young woman. "It would be so nice to have twins."

"No," said Emil. "We can't take but the one. So make up your mind which. We got a long ride ahead of us and we can't waste no more time."

"Well . . ." said his wife. And then the decision was made for her. A bubble of gas pressed somewhere inside Herbert and, stiffening, he began to yell.

"Not *that* one," said Emil Schwimmbeck.

Within the hour, Otto was bouncing north in his new mother's arms. No papers had been signed, but in those simpler days, signings were not always required. This was not an adoption. It was, rather, an acquisition, and therefore far less formal.

Herbert, returned alone to his crib, continued to yell, though the fateful bubble of gas had long since passed away. He was miserable without knowing why, and he yelled until at last Clarissa, appearing suddenly, loomed over the crib and shouted, "Quit that!" Stunned, Herbert paused and blinked. And then, exhausted, he fell asleep abruptly.

Clarissa was so pleased by her newly discovered power that she turned at once maternal. She moved the baby from the side of the crib, where he had huddled, into the center, and spread an unnecessary blanket over him. "There, sweetheart, see? You can have the whole thing to yourself now," she cooed.

But in less than ten minutes Herbert had managed in his sleep to inch himself back to his own side again. He had no conception of middles, and did not know, then or ever afterward, that he was whole all by himself, instead of half of a single unit.

Wednesday, May 21, 1952

Babe and Louisa sit side by side, with Babe at the wheel, in Aunt Opal's Oldsmobile. They have dropped Aunt Opal off for her regular Wednesday bridge and now they are going to Bell Fountain, the only town of any size near Mussel Point. They are wearing today, by prearrangement, their little green print with the kick pleat. Why "little" should pertain, neither of them knows, especially since, in the size they take, the yardage is substantial; but that's what the Higbee's ad in the Sunday *Plain Dealer* said it was—they always get a Cleveland paper on Sundays. The ad called it "an important little print," and, easily convinced, they ordered two. By telephone. They seldom go in person up to Cleveland; a trip to Bell Fountain, twelve miles away, is quite enough of an adventure.

The Oldsmobile is long and black and looks official, and so it was once, in a way. It belonged at first to their uncle, Dr. Stuart Loose; was new, in fact, two months before he died; a sleek and costly car, thanks to the volatile health of the Mussel Point community. He barely got out of it, that day five years ago, in time to have his ringingly decisive heart attack. Right there on the flagstones leading to his own front door, beside the winter-brown azaleas with their curled-up leaves, he curled up, himself, and went down for the count, his medical bag with its useful clutter, though no use at all in this instance, intact at his side when they found him.

The Oldsmobile is Aunt Opal's now, unrestricted. She likes it much better than the Studebaker that was hers when Stuart died, because it has "fluid drive" and she doesn't have to shift. She gave the Studebaker to Walter right after the funeral, but now it is someone else's. Walter traded it in at once. It had a peculiar shape and the color—gray—didn't suit him. It looked, he said, "too much like Mother," adding hastily that he only meant it looked like something only a mother would own.

Babe drives cautiously out of Mussel Point, and turns southeast toward Bell Fountain. "This car scares me to death," she confesses to Louisa. "The hood's so different from Daddy's Lincoln, it's hard to judge how wide it is."

"I know," says Louisa. "And it's funny not to have to shift."

"That's the thing," says Babe. "I never know what to do with my other foot."

"Want me to drive?" Louisa offers.

"No, that's all right. I'll just go slow, if you don't mind."

"*I* don't mind," says Louisa comfortably. "Go as slow as you want. I'm just glad to get out of the house."

A mile beyond Mussel Point, Babe says, "There's the greenhouse."

"There it is," agrees Louisa.

Off to the left, behind a roomy gravel turnaround, stands a long, low, fragile-looking building made of glass, fronted by a small clapboard showroom. A friendly sign above the door announces that this is Festeen's Nursery, and another sign on a banner in a window says: *Festeen's for Greens.*

"Mr. Festeen's in the hospital again," says Babe.

"I know," says Louisa. "Daddy said something about it at breakfast."

Mr. Festeen is their father's oldest friend, a partner for years at the Pleasure Dome but now long retired and living with his son on the farm that rolls away behind the greenhouse.

"Maybe we should have asked Daddy if he wanted to go along to Bell Fountain," says Babe. "We could have run him over to the hospital for a visit."

"Babe, I *did* ask him," says Louisa, "and you know what he said? He said, 'Dick's got so old and tottery it makes me sick to look at him.'"

"Oh, Louisa, he didn't! That's a terrible thing to say about your best friend!"

"Well, it's just what I was telling you yesterday,

Babe. He's so touchy this last day or two, I'm almost afraid to speak to him."

The greenhouse drops away behind as they think this over. Babe negotiates a chicken who, the proverb notwithstanding, is not trying to cross the road but merely wishes to investigate the berm. Still, chickens are unpredictable. The pass accomplished, Babe says, "Well, there's no excuse for it. After all, Mr. Festeen is almost eighty. Daddy ought to be glad he's still around. Why, they've been friends forever!"

Louisa says, "Not so much the last few years, though."

Babe slows, takes a hand from the wheel, and rolls down her window to the light May air. "Is he still acting funny?" she asks.

"He said he had a headache this morning," Louisa reports. "And he's still squinting with that one eye. I don't think he looks well at all."

"Glasses," Babe suggests. "Maybe he's gotten to the point he needs his glasses changed."

"That could be it," says Louisa. "We'd better make him an appointment." She lifts the hem of the little green print and flaps it up and down, revealing plump knees that are mottled from the pressure of taut-stretched nylons and early heat. "Whew!" she says. "I'm roasting. Did you ask Aunt Opal about the surprise party?"

"Yes," says Babe, "and she said she thought he'd hate it. And *then* she said, 'Don't you girls know by now your father hates everything he's not in charge of?' "

"Oh, dear," says Louisa.

"Well, they never did get along very well," says Babe.

"I know, but you'd think for his birthday . . ."

"Oh," says Babe, "she doesn't mind giving the dinner. She just thinks a surprise would be silly."

"Well, I suppose maybe he *wouldn't* like it," says Louisa with a sigh.

"Probably not," says Babe. "Well, never mind. Where shall we look first when we get to Bell Fountain?"

"*I* don't know," says Louisa. "Daddy's the hardest person I know to buy presents for. There's never anything he needs."

They think this over also, as they must twice a year. It is a problem so immense that every Christmas, every birthday, is blighted by it.

The car rolls smoothly between the shabby farms softened now with late spring bloom, and then Louisa says, "Look—look at that billboard."

There is a sign ahead plastered with a poster that cries COLE BROTHERS CIRCUS in huge red letters, and adds in orange: *Coming Soon.* Below this is a picture of a lion leaping toward them through a hoop of flame, leaping right out of the sign, almost, his terrible jaws wide open on a roar. The blazing tropical colors of the sign eclipse the May of the countryside, the great exotic head of the lion with his glittering fangs implies that nothing ever happens in Ohio.

Babe says, "Not after *last* year." And with no more than these four words she acknowledges the fondness Herbert Rowbarge has for lions—not real ones, perhaps, but certainly the pair on the merry-go-round at the Pleasure Dome—and reminds Louisa that, the year before, they gave him for his birthday a little gold lion for his watch chain, a real gold charm to replace the one he's always worn there, a wooden one so paintless and thumbed and blunt that it scarcely looks like a lion at all any more. He has put the gold one away somewhere and continues to wear the wooden one—a measure of their usual success in giving him presents.

"I guess you're right," says Louisa, and they leave the billboard—and Africa's advantages—behind.

The signs are thicker suddenly, making a noise on both sides of the road. Amid the clamor of announcements of products available ahead, one sign declares with pride: *Highest Point in the State—1549 Feet above Sea Level.* And another demands that they *Visit Zane Caverns.* They have never been to the sea and have no interest in its level as compared to their own. Nor have they seen Zane Caverns, which sound all damp and full of bats. But the products announced are delightful, and so is the small, more modest sign at a crossroads: *Bell Fountain 2 Miles.*

"Oh, good," says Babe. "Look, let's order some flowers for Mr. Festeen, and then go have a soda. I'm so dry I could . . ."

"Spit rust," they say together, and laugh.

"What about Daddy, though?" Louisa reminds her.

"Well," says Babe, "maybe a bathrobe or something."

"All right," says Louisa, relieved. "He won't like what we give him, anyway."

"No," Babe agrees. "But it's not our fault. There's nothing in the world he *needs*."

Summer 1882

For Herbert, the second year of life was full of events. In May, two of his three daily playmates, Anna and Charles, were acquired and taken away. In July, the other playmate, Lizzie, turned six and was absorbed into the older girls' activities. His world remained solitary, except for Clarissa, for a period of several weeks, and then, all on the same day in August, a box of used toys arrived from Gaitsburg, a new boy was brought to the Home, and Clarissa of the blasphemous tongue, Clarissa the domineering nursemaid, Clarissa at the age of thirteen disappeared.

Though Herbert did not know it, Clarissa had run away, and no one had been able to find her. By eluding the Gaits County sheriff and escaping thereby the terrible punishment meted out to returned runaways, she became a kind of hero to the other children. But Herbert at the time knew only that Clarissa was not there in the morning, and that later, after a long, cranky day alone in the nursery, he was given his supper by someone new. And it was this new boy who opened the box of secondhand toys at bedtime and brought forth a Noah's Ark.

When Herbert saw the Noah's Ark, when it was put into his hands, he forgot Clarissa at once. Poor Clarissa! Running, stumbling, running again along the dark banks of the Ohio all through the August night! To be forgotten for a wooden Noah's Ark!

Poor Clarissa? Nonsense. She stowed away on a riverboat, stole a handsome little dress and shoes right out of a sleeping young passenger's cabin, slipped off in St. Louis, and found work as a maid in a rich man's house where later she wooed and won the rich man's nephew and moved to Wichita to live in style with a housemaid of her own. No love lost either way: she had forgotten little Herbert on the very first night, somewhere between Portsmouth and Cincinnati.

The new boy's name was Dick Festeen, and he took an immediate shine to Herbert. He was a simple boy with simple needs, and he needed Herbert quite simply to save his sanity.

Early in the spring, the flood-swollen waters of Possum Creek, snarling down to the Ohio southwest of Gaitsburg, had crested suddenly and snatched a thin old bridge right out from under the wagon in which were riding Dick and his mother and father and his little brother, Frank. All were swept away and drowned except for Dick and the horse, and since that accident, which had taken place in March, Dick—and the horse—had been boarding with friends of the family. But as summer came to an end, the friends found themselves unable to see how they could provide winter food and clothing for an extra child. With regret and relief, they delivered Dick to the Children's Home and went away sighing. They did, however, find themselves able to keep the horse.

Dick Festeen missed his father and mother deeply, but his real anguish was for the loss of his brother, Frank. It was an act of God, the family friends had said—to soothe him—and at one level he was able to accept this explanation. Still, it was hard, sometimes, to understand why God had seen fit to tumble such a little child away under the wild brown water while Dick, so clearly flailing and thrashing to save him, was so clearly praying that the little child be spared.

It was very hard, and Dick was sore of soul on the evening he was brought to the Children's Home. He had not smiled since March, and his ten-year-old body, lately so rosy and strapping, was visibly dwindling. But Mrs. Frate, on hearing his story from the family friends, was wise. She sent him at once to the nursery. The skills he had acquired through caring for his brother were needed there, anyway—Clarissa had run away the night before.

It was a happy thing to do. Seeing Herbert, the

new boy smiled. By bedtime he was Herbert's slave, and when the Noah's Ark was produced, the friendship was cemented. Mrs. Frate, allowing him to sleep that night in the nursery with Herbert, gave Dick the first good rest he had had in many weeks. The Lord taketh away, to be sure, but the Lord also giveth. A healing had begun for Dick Festeen.

Herbert knew nothing of the new boy's story till long afterward. At the time, on that August night in 1882, he was glad to have Dick's company, but far more than that, he was entranced by the Noah's Ark.

This toy, once bright with paint, and with all its pairs of animals intact, had belonged to the hard-eyed daughter of a Gaitsburg minister. After a few short weeks of possession, she had managed to destroy the hinge which allowed its roof to open and close, had scraped away most of the color from its hull, and had lost Mr. and Mrs. Noah and half the animals. All this had been done deliberately—several of the missing animals were discovered later, buried in the soil of a potted fern—because she had wanted instead, from a catalogue, a dollhouse of particularly rich design which made her father, the minister, uneasy. It had furniture upholstered in red velvet, and a lot of gold enamel, and it made him think of sin. So he gave her the Noah's Ark as a substitute, and when she had completed its ruin, he took it away from her and gave it to the Children's Home—to punish her, he said. But of course she was delighted, and of course, later, she got the dollhouse she had wanted in the first place, and a lovely set of dolls to go with it.

The Lord taketh away, but the Lord also giveth. Herbert was much moved by the Noah's Ark without for a moment knowing why. When it reached his hands, it still had seven of its little wooden animals: twin camels, twin elephants, twin bears, and one lonely lion that had lost its twin forever.

Thursday, May 22, 1952

Louisa Rowbarge sits on her bed in the room that, nearly all their lives, she has shared with Babe. It is a pretty room, carpeted in blue, with yellow roses on the wallpaper and yellow bedspreads of the type known as chenille, with tiny tufts of cotton yarn pulled through the fabric to trace a geometric pattern. Most of the time Louisa likes the bedspreads, but this morning she knows they will give her trouble: she has a present to wrap, and experience has taught her that it's hard to wrap presents on a soft and knobby surface. The dining-room table would be better, but she can't do it there; Herbert Rowbarge is afoot downstairs and would be sure to see.

Beside Louisa on the bed is an oblong box of flimsy cardboard labeled *Boyd's of Bell Fountain—Wearables for Men*, which cradles, in slick tissue, a crisp new seersucker bathrobe folded just so, its tags and pins removed, ready to be lifted out and exclaimed over. Louisa takes the lid from the box for a final look, and sighs. What will he say when he sees it, she wonders: "Oh, this is grand," or "Oh, another bathrobe"? The bathrobe seemed like a good idea yesterday, but now she's not so sure.

Footsteps on the staircase warn her that her father is no longer on the first floor, but coming up. She freezes, the box lid on her lap, and waits. The footsteps come along the hall outside her door, and anxiously she cries, "Daddy? Don't come in!"

The footsteps pause. "What?" he says. "Is that you, Babe?"

"*Louisa*, Daddy. Don't you dare come in." This last girlishly, with a nervous little giggle.

After a moment he says, dryly, "My God. What's the matter? Are you entertaining a lover? Never mind. I don't want to come in."

The footsteps move away and she hears him go into his own room, into the bathroom that is his alone. There is the sound of running water, then silence. Aspirin, she thinks; he's taking aspirin again. And then—a sudden, sharp sound that makes her jump—glass shattering on the hard tile floor. She leaps up, goes to her door, and puts her head out. "Daddy?" she calls. "Are you all right?" There is no answer, and she calls again, "*Daddy?*"

At last he says, sounding surprised, "I broke the tumbler. It jumped right out of my hand."

"Oh, Daddy, that's too bad," she says. "Well, leave it where it is. I'll clean it up in a minute. Don't you try—you'll cut yourself." She hears him come out of his bathroom, and shuts her door hastily.

He pauses again in the hall outside and says, still sounding surprised, "That was the damnedest thing, the way it just—dropped."

"That's all right," she says through the door. "Everyone does that once in a while."

He is silent for a moment and then he says, "I suppose so. Well, I'm going down to the park now, Babe."

She opens her mouth to correct him again, decides against it, and says, "All right, Daddy. Be careful."

"Of what?" he asks.

"I just meant—oh, *you* know, just be *careful.* It doesn't mean anything. Will you be back for lunch?"

"I don't know," he says. "Maybe."

She hears his footsteps on the stairs—slow footsteps, as if he were being careful after all—and she thinks to herself, he's old, he sounds so old. Soon the garage door below her window grumbles up its track, the Lincoln coughs gently and begins to murmur. She crosses the room and peers down as the car backs into the turnaround and heads out the driveway.

She feels lighthearted, suddenly, with her father gone. The house expands, seems almost conspiratorial. And then, remembering the bathrobe, she goes back to the bed and looks at it. The sense of doubt returns. But it's too late now. She replaces the lid, which goes down with a flatulent *pooh,* and picks up a long roll of wrapping paper. She's not so sure about the paper, either. The choice was between a roll with different kinds of pipes printed on it and "Dad" repeated over and over in brown and tan, and this one, the one they settled on, with puppies; a friendlier paper somehow, the puppies all roly-poly, tangled up in the words "Happy Birthday" spelled out in curling green ribbon. There is real green ribbon made to match, and it was this added feature that tipped the balance. But now—"Oh, dear," she says aloud, and wishes Babe were there. When she and Babe are together, everything seems easy, everything makes sense. Alone, she is sure of nothing. The planet may slide at any moment from its orbit, the sun lurch sidewise, the carpeting break free from its moorings with a *whump* and roll itself thickly up to smother her.

She spreads out a length of paper from its cardboard tube, and while she reaches for the scissors, it curls back up again slyly. She thinks of the carpeting—waiting, she knows, to do the same—and gives it a suspicious glance, but it keeps all innocent and blue to the floor, muffling its intent.

This fear of being squeezed to death by carpeting is unique to her—Babe isn't bothered by it—and seems to stem from a series of childhood nightmares having to do somehow with being born; this she has gleaned from reading, surreptitiously, Freud's *Interpretation of Dreams*. Louisa rather likes having a mild neurosis—especially the fact that it's unique—except for when, on rare occasions, the nightmares make a reappearance. At times like that, she finds she'd just as soon avoid the kind of store where carpeting is sold, or where, beneath high ceilings with fluorescent lights, she will be apt to see, standing against a wall, great towering tunnels of menacing linoleum. Babe always laughs at her anxiety, but then she can say, and always does, in a solemn, righteous tone, "You were born *first*, Babe. Everything was easy for *you*."

Now, scissors in hand, tape at the ready, she spreads out the paper once more and at last the box is wrapped, secured by its ribbon in a loopy bow. "There!" says Louisa, and with the scissors she clips the ribbon ends smartly, at an angle. At least, she thinks, the *box* looks nice. Still, puppies—he'll probably think it's silly. Well, if he does, he does. She and Babe have done the best they can.

She picks up the box and stands for a moment, puzzling. Where to hide it? It must, of course, be hidden. She knows he has no interest in his birthday, that it would never occur to him to go searching for presents, but hiding the box is part of the ritual. It will make her feel better to think of the bathrobe tucked away in some shadowy place, waiting for the big day.

The closet. Of course. She crosses the room, sees her reflection coming toward her in the long glass on the closet door, and pauses. She forgets in between, and is reminded repeatedly as she moves every day around her room, how comforting it is to see herself this way. It's as if Babe were there with her after all. She lifts a hand to tuck a stray curl back into its bobby pin and beams at Babe–Louisa, who beams back reassuringly. Then she opens the closet door and, on tiptoe, tilts the present onto an upper shelf, behind a hatbox and a heating pad. Maybe he *will* like it, she thinks, and then—yes, I'm sure he will. She closes the door and, humming, leaves the room and goes to clean up the broken bathroom tumbler.

Winter 1883

The love and attention lavished on him by Dick Festeen gave Herbert's life a new dimension, one he quickly came to take for granted. For the Home continued crowded, so that Mrs. Frate continued to allow Dick to sleep in the nursery, and this meant that the two were together night and day. True, the Home was new—that is to say, it was ten years old—but almost at once it had proved to be inadequate.

Built by a well-intentioned citizen of means, one Henry Wesseldine, and received with gratitude, since the need was great, the Home was also pointed to with pride—for Wesseldine, in the manner of the times, had spared not a thing but convenience. The building, attended by a barn and sheds, stood solid and imposing on top of its knobby little hill—one hill of hundreds bestowed, it is said, by the glacier on the otherwise simple surface of southeastern Ohio —and it was built to last, with foundations of white-washed boulders and walls of smooth gray stone.

Inside, the ceilings were lofty, the windows as tall as the doors, and every room had a fireplace with a gracious mantel and moldings. In the wide entrance hall, a splendid staircase fanned up to the second floor between oak banisters, and rich red carpeting softened its steps.

But this, after all, was nothing but a shell. Wesseldine, for all his generosity, had provided no money for furnishings. These were donations, and looked it, and more than that, were too scant to relieve an all-pervasive hollowness. The kitchen was in the cellar, which made it convenient only for the rats. The privies were outside at a distance arrived at by compromise: too far in the winter, too near in the summer. And in the bedrooms upstairs, conceived for twenty children, thirty-two were housed in that winter of '83.

The floor was divided in halves, front and back, with the nursery between. The front half, encircling the stairwell, was for the girls. The back half, with its own stairway—steep, dark, and free of carpeting —was for the boys. Each had two rooms with rows of narrow cots—five to a room, of course, in that curious way we have of assuming that Nature will be evenhanded. Once or twice there really had been twenty children to sleep in them, but they came and went, their number always changing, and in ten years they had never once been equally divided as to sex.

In 1883, the proportion was particularly lopsided: eighteen boys, not counting Dick and Herbert, and an even dozen girls. So it was crowded on the second floor, especially for the boys, with extra cots squeezed in every which way and such total confusion at bedtime that the pale Mrs. Frate turned paler with every passing month. So Dick had a cot in the nursery, where he vastly preferred to be, and Herbert's little life was the luckier for it. He was given his way in everything, and time passed with only one significant event.

The doors at the Home—all the doors—were kept locked. Otherwise, the children opened them—to poach from the icebox and the storeroom, to visit back and forth between the girls' half floor and the boys', to poke around in Mrs. Frate's big desk among such skimpy records as were kept there, or—to run away. So Mrs. Frate kept her keys in her apron pocket. The cook, Mrs. Daigle, kept another set in hers. No one else was ever allowed to unlock doors except for the handyman, who was responsible for all repairs and all the heaviest chores. And the handyman was sometimes careless.

His name was Mr. Buzzey, and one morning in January, while Dick was attending a class in the schoolroom, Mr. Buzzey swayed up the central staircase and let himself into the nursery to mend a broken cupboard hinge. Herbert came near to oversee this work, full of questions and advice, but Mr.

Buzzey ignored him in preference to singing, in a tender monotone, a popular song of the time, an appropriate song called "There Is a Tavern in the Town." There *was* a tavern in the town, as Mr. Buzzey had reason to know. In fact, there were several, including the establishment operated by Mr. and Mrs. Mink in the very building where Herbert had been born. Mr. Buzzey sang of it now with affection, and when the cupboard hinge was fixed, more or less, he went away still singing, through the door to the upstairs hall, leaving that door wide open. And after a moment's hesitation Herbert came up to it like Alice to the rabbit hole, took ten steps straight ahead, and fell down the central staircase.

Loose-boned by virtue of his youth, and cushioned by the carpeting, Herbert arrived at the bottom without breaking. He was shaken, of course, but he did not cry, for two years with Clarissa had taught him that crying did more harm than good. He merely sat up, rubbing his head, and looked around. And as his eyes turned left, to the wall opposite the matron's office door, he froze in an ecstasy of terror and delight. There was another child sitting at the bottom of another staircase, and that child was wearing the same shirt and trousers and was rubbing his head, too. Herbert Rowbarge had discovered mirrors.

With no one to know that he was there, since Dick was still in the schoolroom and Mrs. Frate was counting linens in the kitchen, Herbert stayed a full half hour in the entrance hall, perfectly content. For not only did the boy in the mirror move as he moved, and make the same faces, this boy was the possessor of the other lion from the Noah's Ark. He brought it out from a pocket just as Herbert was producing his own, and when Herbert pressed his lion to the surface of the glass, the other boy did the same, so that the two little wooden animals were together again at last. Herbert smiled at the boy in the mirror, and the boy smiled back, and the time they spent together in the entrance hall was a time of sweet discovery and peace.

He was found at last by Mrs. Frate, and some sense of his pleasure must have radiated from him, for she paused a moment, watching, loath to disturb him. And then, when she went to him to pick him up, he saw with a start that another Mrs. Frate was picking up his newfound friend, and both began to shriek with rage, to be separated so. Only after her promise that he could come again and play there did Herbert allow himself to be carried away at last, and even so, she had to bring him back twice over to make sure the other boy still clutched the long-lost other lion and was there to wave goodbye.

True to her word, she brought him, once or twice, to play again by the mirror. But his shrieks when the periods were over so convulsed him that Mrs. Frate decided it was bad for his constitution. After that, he stayed in the nursery, and, after that, it was easy to make him angry.

In the daytime, that is, it was easy. Crossed, he would scowl at Dick, refuse to eat his supper, and keep to himself as much as he could. But at night, in bed, protected by the darkness, he would bring the lion out from under his pillow and turn it over and over in his fingers. Then, sleeping at last, he would have a dream which was to come to him now and again for many months thereafter.

He would find himself arm in arm with the boy in the entrance-hall mirror. They would smile at each other, and float off together into a world that was neither the world of the mirror nor any other place he knew, but a far more magical place, a dim and watery place with little boats, a warm place far away. This was all that happened in the dream, but, dreaming it, he was eased. In the morning he would waken calm and cheerful, and the anger sometimes did not come back till long after breakfast.

Friday, May 23, 1952

Babe and Louisa Rowbarge are walking down Lake Street toward the President McKinley Tea Room. On their right they pass a series of frumpy little stands —you could hardly call them shops—which will soon, in a week, throw open their shutters and do a brisk business all summer long in bathing caps, postcards, painted tin buckets and shovels, straw hats, sunglasses, and all manner of glossy trash, most of it labeled *RED MAN LAKE* or *MUSSEL POINT, OHIO*, and all of it made in Japan. On their left is the broad brown lake itself, its shore here toothed with docks where bob all kinds of watercraft, from rowboats-by-the-hour to knife-prowed motorboats, privately owned, with lacquered decks and gleaming chrome—motorboats with cryptic names like *Ten O'Clock* and *No One Home* as well as the more expectable *Suzy-Q*. The motorboats look scrubbed and tidy, the rowboats less so, with their oars standing up on end, jumbled into dockside racks like pick-up-sticks, just as the rowboats themselves are jumbled sometimes as many as ten at a single dock, their sides bumping hollowly, their green or gray paint scuffed and peeling. But all of them look inviting.

"I love summer," says Babe.

"Me, too," says Louisa.

Ahead, where the banks of the lake curve sharply to the left, rises the long inner fence of the Pleasure Dome, right at the water's edge. But there is a wide break, halfway along the fence, where, they know, there is a pavilion soon to be scattered with wooden benches and tables. Here you can sit and eat your hot dogs and your popcorn—or recover from your nausea incurred on the Tilt-A-Wheel—and look at the water before going back for one more ride on something safe like the Bumper Cars or the merry-go-round.

"We're lucky to live in a place like this," says Louisa. "It's so much *fun*."

"I know," says Babe. "I always think that. What if Daddy'd been a lawyer or something? What if he'd stayed in Cincinnati?"

"I know," says Louisa, and repeats, humbly, "We're lucky."

Everything is polished today, or in the process of getting that way, and Babe and Louisa are no exception. They have just spent two hours at Miriam's House of Beauty and are redolent with lotions, their curls so tight around their heads that it seems they must still be wearing the thick-webbed hairnets which are *de rigueur* for under-the-dryer at Miriam's. This loving attention to their scalps has left them drowsy, and the sun flashing on the water, the smell of warm, wet wood that rises from the docks, and the cheerful anticipation all around them of the season's opening, all this makes them feel rich and favored. They would hold hands and skip along the sidewalk, as they used to do when they were children, but for the certainty that everyone would laugh at them. The deference they are shown on the streets of Mussel Point—for being their father's daughters— is too valuable to risk; it is the only deference they get. So they walk, demurely, in their "blue linen frock with the modified sailor collar." Clothes, for Babe and Louisa, are always in the singular—"our blue linen sailor," "our little green print"—as if they were both always zipped together into a single costume.

"I wrapped the bathrobe," says Louisa.

"Oh, good," says Babe. "How does it look?"

"All right, but I hope he doesn't think the paper's silly."

"He won't even notice it," says Babe.

They pass the dance hall, on their left, a structure that is little more than a peaking roof on posts, built out on stilts over the water, where two boys are twisting new bulbs into long strings of lights that will illuminate its rafters and its eaves and make a heaven for moths and dancers alike. And on their right they pass the Mussel Point Inn, all white clapboard and smart black shutters, set back behind a deep half circle of gravel driveway, its wide veranda bare still of the ferns and rocking chairs that are its normal summer decoration. A woman is sweeping the steps, a man rakes the gravel.

"Company coming," says Babe.

Louisa laughs delightedly. "That's clever, Babe," she says. "That's exactly what it's like."

They arrive at the tea room's path just in time to hear, from behind the locked gates of the Pleasure Dome, a sudden burst of strident, tinny music. "Listen, Babe," says Louisa. "They're testing the merry-go-round."

They stand on the sidewalk, listening, and then Babe says, "Daddy's in there, I suppose."

"Of course he is," says Louisa. "He was all excited this morning, just like a little boy. They're trying out a few new tunes today, and of course he wouldn't miss *that.*"

"One thing you can say for Daddy," says Babe, "he really loves his work."

"Yes," says Louisa, "he really does. It's kind of touching, don't you think so?"

"I guess," says Babe. "It's funny, though. Daddy's a funny duck. You'd think a man who got so much pleasure out of a merry-go-round would be a different kind of person. You know, kind of jolly and laughing a lot. But Daddy—well, you'd certainly never describe him as jolly."

Louisa thinks this over, and at last she says, "He's been happy, though, I think. Don't you think he's been happy?"

"He's always had everything," says Babe. "Why shouldn't he be happy? Come on, let's get our treat. I'm starved."

And side by side they disappear into the President McKinley Tea Room.

Summer 1889

When Herbert Rowbarge was nine, an event of huge significance occurred which brought his childhood to a close and defined his future for him, though there were still another nine long years remaining before he left the Home. He had grown, and Dick had managed to remain at his side. Neither was acquired or adopted. For Herbert, at nine, had become too narrow of frame, too sharp of eye. Though it was clear that he was smart, it was also clear that he was used to his own way. Dick had seen to that. And then there was that anger in him, too, always ready to explode. These very qualities, in fact, had prompted the cook, Mrs. Daigle, to suggest the surname Rowbarge for him. And though this last had occurred some three years earlier, it is worth recording.

Mrs. Daigle had an ear for names. She knew what sounded nice with what. And she knew a great many people, in the county and elsewhere, which gave her a large store of names from which to choose. So when, one morning, Mrs. Frate gave up with a sigh and admitted to herself that Herbert was unlikely to gain a name by adoption, she took the matter into her own hands and went, as usual, to the cook for consultation.

"Hmm," said Mrs. Daigle, brushing flour from her elbows. "A last name for Bertie? Let's go and have a look at him. A name's got to match a person."

So they went to the schoolroom and looked at Herbert while pretending to look at something else, and then, back in the kitchen, Mrs. Daigle took up her rolling pin, gestured with it, and said, "Rowbarge. That's the name. That child is a dead ringer for a boy named Rowbarge I used to know that worked for my uncle over to Chillicothe. Skinny, light-brown hair, long nose, and that sharp way of looking at you. And it sounds good with Herbert, seems to me."

"Rowbarge," said Mrs. Frate slowly, trying it out. "Herbert Rowbarge. Yes, it does sound right, somehow. Very well, Rowbarge it shall be. Thank you, Mrs. Daigle."

"Don't mention it," said the cook.

Mrs. Frate turned to go, and then she paused and turned back. "Mrs. Daigle, you don't suppose . . . that is, if Herbert looks so much like this young man you used to know, do you think it's possible he might be . . ."

Mrs. Daigle shook her head. "No," she said, "Bob Rowbarge got hisself shot at Gettysburg in '63. Never had time to get married, even, let alone get some girl in trouble on the side. Anyways, that was long before Bertie was born."

"Yes—well—I just wondered," said Mrs. Frate. "Do you think the family will mind if Herbert borrows their name?"

"Not them!" said Mrs. Daigle. "Bunch of thieves and lowlifes, most of 'em. Lived up near Wheeling, as I recall, or *somewhere* off. They hanged two or three of 'em and the rest run off out West. Bob was the only one with any sense. No, they won't mind. Go ahead. Herbert Rowbarge—it's got a real nice ring to it."

Getting a name was important, but it was not so significant by half as what happened in the summer of '89. In the late summer of every year, the waters of the Ohio River dwindled and stayed low till well into the autumn. A system of dams had been planned to correct this problem and that of the annual flooding; in fact, a flood in '84 had carried away large parts of Gaitsburg, including not only Mink's Saloon but Mr. and Mrs. Mink themselves and the barrel of beer they were gallantly trying to salvage. So the dams had seemed like a good idea, and the first of the series had been finished up near Pittsburgh in '85. But then the money grew scarcer and scarcer, with railway construction gobbling up so much of

WITHDRAWN

it, and anyway, in '89 a lot of people changed their minds about the virtues of dams. Over in Pennsylvania, at the end of May, a dam outside Johnstown had collapsed, and the waters of the Conemaugh had lunged out and drowned two thousand people. A toll like that was impressive, and Johnstown was not that far away. So the summer in question saw the great Ohio as shallow as ever, and as difficult for shipping. Shipping, nevertheless, continued. And once in a while a boat would go aground, or get hung up on a snag. This, then, is how there came to be a merry-go-round set up in a field outside Gaitsburg one bright, hot morning in July.

Herbert heard the music when he went out that morning to lead the Home's three cows to pasture. He had heard little enough music of any kind in his life, but even to the local connoisseurs, such as they were, this music was special: shrill as a whistle, even at a distance, and altogether merry and devil-may-care. It came to Herbert's ears imperiously, demanding his attention. He hurried the cows on their way and ran back to see if he could find where it was coming from.

In the driveway he met Mr. Buzzey, just arriving for his day's work, and Mr. Buzzey, too, was wide of eye and openmouthed. "Y'hear that?" he wheezed excitedly, seizing on a very willing Herbert to bless with the news. "That's what they call a merry-go-round, *that* is. Barge went aground last night. They're workin' now to get 'er loose. But it was bringin' this here merry-go-round down, made all the way up to Buffalo, can ya beat that?—fella got a factory up there makes 'em—and they're takin' 'er clear out to St. Louie! So they figured they better get 'er off the barge, case she turned over, and they got 'er set up and runnin' sweet as you please right down in the yard back of the stables."

"Where? Where?" cried Herbert, straining uselessly on tiptoe to peer between the trees on the plain below.

"Can't see 'er from here," said Mr. Buzzey cruelly. "Say, she's a beauty! Got all these here big animals goes round and round and up and down, horses and tigers and everything, painted up bright and shiny, and a big red canvas top on 'er, and a steam organ, and she's smokin' and blowin' like nobody's business. They're gonna run 'er all day and take in a pile of money. Costs a nickel to ride 'er, but even so, half the people in town is down there lined up, waitin' for a turn. I ain't got a nickel, just at the moment, or I swear I'da had me a ride myself."

"Maybe we'll get to go down!" Herbert exclaimed, trying to picture the machine in his imagination and finding it far too exotic.

"You crazy or somethin'?" Mr. Buzzey demanded. "You got about as much chance a' seein' that merry-go-round as you got seein' Jack the Ripper. Boy, it's a wonder, durned if it ain't!" And he wandered off, still gesturing, and marveling under his breath.

There was a plaque in the schoolroom which read: "The consciousness of duty performed gives us music at midnight." But Herbert had no intention of waiting till midnight for his music. He wanted it now. Early that afternoon, weeding in the garden side by side with Dick, he said in a low voice, "Let's sneak out and go take a look at that merry-go-round."

"Gosh, Bertie, how we gonna do that?" Dick said, astonished. "Somebody'd see us, sure, and you know what'd happen then." Dick, at seventeen, was large and slow-moving, with a great sheaf of straight yellow hair that hung over his eyebrows; but the gray eyes below were gentle and serious and, when they gazed at Herbert, full of tenderness. They were, now, full of apprehension, too, for he knew how determined his adopted little brother could be.

"Look here," said Herbert. "Pretty soon we got to go pick berries out back of the barn. We can sneak off then. Nobody'll notice, not if we're careful."

"We-ell, maybe, but what if they did? I don't care for *me* so much, but gee whiz, Bertie, you're too little to—"

"I am not!" Herbert interrupted with heat. "I *got* to see that merry-go-round, no matter what. You can come if you want, or you can stay. I don't care. But I'm goin'."

"Gee whiz, Bertie," Dick said helplessly. He paused, looking at the stern young face that stared back at him so impatiently. "Well . . . gee whiz, I can't let you go alone."

"You can, too!" Herbert exclaimed. The anger that was always just beneath the surface turned his thin cheeks red, and he scowled. "You got to quit callin' me a baby."

"I didn't call you a baby, Bertie," Dick protested. "*I* know you're not a—"

"Well, that's right," said Herbert. "So do what you want. I'm goin' down."

They went together.

It was easy enough to do, at that. Easy to slip away down the hill behind the barn, to circle around and come in to Gaitsburg from behind, drawn by the music like the Magi by the Star of Bethlehem. Herbert knew as well as Dick what would happen if someone caught them. But the music drove all apprehension from his mind. It called him and he had to go.

And oh, how wonderful it was! The field behind the stables was jammed with people, but the bright canvas top of the merry-go-round thrust up far over their heads, and the richly tinny music, loud as a brass band, drowned out their babble, even drowned out, almost, the clanking of the machinery. Black smoke billowed up into the sky, swirling when a breeze caught it, and dropping soot on everyone below, but nobody seemed to mind.

Herbert made his way determinedly through the crowd, with Dick close behind him, and then—it stood revealed to him in all its magnificence, and it

was, he saw at once, a glorious, enormous Noah's
Ark. There were many pairs of horses, four at least,
but there was, as well, a pair of camels. And two
stags, even two tigers. There were chariots, their
sides carved to look like dragons with handsome,
scaly tails. But best of all, there was a pair of lions—
yes, a pair—their fierce wooden jaws snarling open
to reveal great lolling tongues and gleaming fangs
within. And, oh, the paint glistened so, like oilcloth,
dazzling in every color known to man, and studded
with great glass jewels that winked as they circled by.

In the middle was a thing with a forest of brass
pipes sticking up, built into a sort of little cupola
rich with cupids, wreathed with wooden garlands,
and set with mirrors that flashed reflections of the
turning beasts that ringed it. Here a man in a gay
striped jacket sat at a keyboard and struck out the
notes of a rollicking waltz. He nodded and smiled
and worked his eyebrows up and down as he played,
and with each striking of a key, a little burst of
steam shot with a piercing whistle out of one of the
brass pipes. It was a steam calliope, the heart of the
merry-go-round.

There had never been anything so fine in all the
history of the world. Of this, Herbert was at once
convinced. He stood with his mouth open, scarcely
breathing. It did not occur to him that he might
aspire to mount one of the animals and whirl off
and around, like the screaming, laughing people who
passed in a blur before him—that he might reach

up and out to catch the brass ring that hung at a tempting height from one of the posts supporting the canvas top. He was content just to stand and gaze at the beauty of the lions—their matching manes, their gracious tails, their smartly lifted forepaws and chins. They were side by side, complete. And suddenly tears came to his eyes. Mrs. Frate had said, not long before, that heaven was "our souls' own country evermore." And now, all at once, Herbert saw what the words were getting at. For this was heaven, surely, and it was his soul's own country. He would have one of these machines someday. He would, he must, and that was all there was to it.

He felt at last Dick's hand on his shoulder. "Bertie, we got to go back. *Now.*"

"Not yet," he managed to reply. "Not yet."

It was too late, anyway. For there beside them, suddenly, loomed that stern agent of another heaven, the Gaitsburg minister whose daughter had been first owner of the nursery's Noah's Ark. He had tried, to no avail, to get the merry-go-round shut down, and now he turned his wrath on Dick and Herbert, targets more within his grasp. "I know you boys," he boomed triumphantly. "You've run away from the Home. No struggling, now. I'm marching you back at once."

Herbert and Dick were led to the cellar and chained to one of the great boulders of the building's foundations. The designated spot, equipped for this purpose when the Home was built, was gloomy and damp, with no comfort or amusement. Even the rats left them alone, for one of these had pushed a Mason jar off a shelf and the pack was occupied with feasting on the applesauce that had splattered on the hard dirt floor a few yards away.

Here the criminals must sit for three full days and nights. It was the regulation punishment, and though it grieved her, Mrs. Frate followed it conscientiously. She took them out to the privies every so often, and at mealtimes she brought them the regulation bread and water. But these events made up the whole of their diversions. It would have been a nightmare to endure alone. With two together it was, by a thin margin, bearable.

"It's my fault," said Dick miserably. "I shouldn't of let you go."

"You couldn't of stopped me," Herbert returned. "And I don't care anyway. I'm glad we went." He was thinking still of the merry-go-round, and had long since passed the point where he could speak of it casually. But, at the same time, his head was so full of it that he wanted to talk of nothing else and so he attempted an oblique approach. "What you gonna do when you get outa here?"

"You mean outa the cellar?"

"No, I mean outa *here*. The Home. Where you gonna go? You'll be eighteen pretty soon. You'll hafta go then—they'll make you."

"I know," said Dick sorrowfully. "I'll get me a job

in Gaitsburg, I guess, so we can sorta stay together. I been thinkin' I'll wait around till you get out and then we can do somethin' together. Start a farm, maybe."

"Not me," said Herbert. "I don't want nothin' to do with any dumb farm."

"Why not?" asked Dick, surprised. "What else you gonna do? Work on the railroad or the river or somethin'?"

Herbert tried to see Dick's face clearly in the gloom, to measure him. He paused, and then decided to risk a partial confession. "Well, I dunno," he said, making an effort to sound offhand. "It might be pretty good to get one of those merry-go-round machines—take it around and run it in the towns, like the one down in Gaitsburg."

Dick paused, himself, considering this proposal. Then he said, gently, "That'd take a whole lot of money, though, Bertie, seems to me."

"Yeah, I guess so," said Herbert.

The merry-go-round was not mentioned again.

After their release from the cellar, Herbert and Dick went along as usual for a time. The merry-go-round was gone, the summer was hot, and everything seemed unchanged. But at the end of August, Dick was summoned to the matron's office and, after a brief conference, emerged and at once sought out Herbert where he wandered in the pasture with the cows.

"Bertie!" he whooped. "I got to go! Right away. Today. Mrs. Frate just found out I turned eighteen last week. But, Bertie, that ain't all. Listen! It turns out they got my father's farm held for me all this time! Some lawyer down in Gaitsburg's been sittin' on the papers—he's my guardian or somethin'—first I knew I *had* a guardian—and Bertie, when I get to twenty-one, I get the farm and everything! I never even thought of it before! Gee whiz, a farm all my own!"

"What you gonna do till you get to twenty-one?" asked Herbert, much impressed.

"Well, gee, I guess get a job in Gaitsburg, like I was gonna do anyhow, save my money, go out to the farm and see what's what," said Dick, his gray eyes large with the wonder of it all. "Bertie, listen, I'll work real hard and then, when you get out, you'll come and live with me. Gee, you never lived nowhere but here, you got no idea what it's like. I can't hardly remember, myself. Listen, I'll send you some money, too, to have all your own. And I'll come and see you all the time. You're my brother, Bertie, and I'm gonna take real good care of you, see if I don't."

And then, overcome with the sudden gift of a future, and his joy in his plans for sharing it, he put his arms around Herbert, hugged him close, and wept.

So the two were parted and that night the cot next to Herbert's was empty. But, instead of feeling lonely,

Herbert went to sleep at once and dreamed, not of Dick, but of the boy in the entrance-hall mirror. And this time, as they floated off smiling together to that dim and watery place so far away, he found that he could hear, just barely, all around them, the music of the merry-go-round.

Saturday, May 24, 1952

Babe and Louisa, on this wet spring morning, meet by accident in an aisle at Ellison's Drug Store. Each wears, tied under the chin, a rain hat, a kind of see-through plastic kerchief strewn with painted daisies, to protect the fresh construction done at Miriam's House of Beauty on the day before. Each carries a yellow umbrella, closed and dangling from a wrist, each wears a rubberized yellow cape designed, by someone clever, to recall the type seen sometimes on policemen. These costumes were intended to be cheerful—they had agreed that yellow was cheerful for stormy days—but the yellow is the yellow of pencils, not butter, and the final effect is violent, the more so for the dim, wet gloom of the morning, which suggests, like church, that something softer would be more respectful.

It is dark outside, more like twilight than morning, and Mr. Ellison has turned on the lights that hang from the ceiling low over every aisle. This makes the rows and rows of bottles, tubes, and boxes seem intimate and cozy, and Babe and Louisa, wandering among them, don't see each other—despite the hard brilliance of their rain gear—till, near a rack of corn pads and thick elastic stockings, they meet face to face. It happens very seldom, a chance encounter like this, and so they pause, gasp, and embrace each other delightedly.

"Oh, Babe, how nice!" Louisa exclaims. "What are *you* doing here?"

Babe holds up a list. "I'm doing cough drops, Vicks, and a new thermometer," she says. "Aunt Opal's decided to have a cold. How about you?"

"I'm getting aspirin," says Louisa. "For Daddy. He takes them all the time now."

"He's still got those headaches?"

"Yes," says Louisa, "and this morning he had a sort of dizzy spell."

"I'm just sure it's his eyes," says Babe. "Remember when Aunt Opal got her bifocals? She was dizzy for a week."

"You're probably right, Babe, but he claims his glasses are fine," says Louisa. "*I* don't know what to do with him."

"Leave him alone," Babe advises. "He's not so old he can't take care of himself."

"I guess so," says Louisa. "But, you know, sometimes I wish Uncle Stuart was still around. It used to be so handy having a doctor in the family. I mean, remember how he could always just casually come over and look at Daddy on the sly?"

"I think Daddy always knew what he was up to, though," says Babe. "Uncle Stuart wasn't the subtlest man in the world."

At the other end of the aisle, a round little figure appears and flaps an arm. "Hoo hoo—Bleeza!" it calls, and hurries toward them. It is Gracie Hannengraff, née Rinehouse, and they have known her all their lives. Today they are happy to see her. Thirty years ago, seeing her filled them with despair. For Gracie was the prettiest girl in the class and, by virtue of her name, was always seated next to them, so that all through school they were made to feel thick and plain and clumsy. However, in the intervening years, Gracie has been rising like bread dough and is now completely spherical. She wears a rain cape, too, today, with a floral design, and resembles a toaster in a cozy. But the nice thing is that Gracie is much more comfortable now than she was before. Thin, she had enemies. Fat, she is loved by everyone. "Bleeza!" she explodes, arriving at the corn-pad rack and bouncing with excitement. "Guess what! Oh, you'll never guess!"

"What?" they say together. "*What?*" They drop easily into the wide-eyed eagerness of their girlhood, just as they accept, without thinking, the name "Bleeza," coined in grammar school by desperate classmates who could never tell them apart and needed a term that meant either or both, to which either or both could answer. It is rather like Boanerges in the Bible; less dramatic, perhaps, but just as handy.

"Tammie's engaged!" gasps Gracie, and at once bursts into tears. "My *baby*! Getting *married*!"

"Oh, Gracie," they say, "that's wonderful! Who's she marrying?"

"Oh, dear," says Gracie, mopping at her face with a handkerchief which looks as if it had done this service several times already in the last hour. "Excuse my blubbering, I'm just so happy. She's engaged to Joe Festeen! Can you believe it?"

"Joe!" says Babe. "How lovely! Is he back from Korea?"

"He only got back yesterday," says Gracie, reaching over her alpine bosom to clasp her little hands at her heart. "And he came right over, all spiffed up in his uniform, and—well—first thing I knew, it was all settled."

"Oh, Gracie," says Louisa, "imagine them being old enough! That makes me feel a hundred."

"Me, too," says Gracie, "but isn't it *fun*? Thank God he came back in one piece, not like his poor grampa. Well, I got to go—but I'm so glad I ran *into* you, Bleeza. I knew you'd be happy to hear the news." And she rolls off down the aisle again and disappears.

"For goodness' sake," says Babe. "Joe Festeen and little Tammie Hannengraff. I can't believe it."

"Gracie'll be a grandmother one of these days,"

says Louisa. "And we're not even a mother. Or an aunt. You'd think Walter would get married, wouldn't you," she adds in exasperation, "instead of larking around the way he does. I *would* like to be an aunt!"

"Well," says Babe, "he certainly won't do it to please *us*. Oh, and that reminds me. Guess what he did do. For Daddy's birthday."

"Oh, dear," says Louisa. "What?"

"He came over last night for supper," says Babe, "and he told me he's hired some man from the air-field down in Dayton to fly over the park and take a picture of it. From *above*. And he's going to have it blown up and framed for Daddy's office. What do you think of that?"

Louisa's mouth has dropped slightly open, her eyes are round. "Oh, Babe! How—imaginative! But that's going to make our bathrobe look sick!"

"I know," says Babe grimly.

They stand for a moment in silence. Outside, there is a sudden blink of lightning and over their heads the long fluorescent bulbs dim briefly and then, with a *snick*, resume their glaring. "Oh, well," says Louisa at last. "We did the best we could."

Together they walk to the front of the store and pay for their purchases, and then they stand at the door, looking out at the rain. "Gracie's fatter than ever," says Louisa.

"I know it," says Babe.

Underneath their rain capes, both suddenly feel thin, and both hearts swell with a love for Gracie that eclipses, for the moment, their annoyance with Walter.

"It's so nice for her," says Louisa. "About Tammie, I mean. I'm really glad."

"Me, too," says Babe. "She looked so happy."

"It's funny," says Louisa generously. "In some ways she's just as pretty as ever."

"Oh, Louisa," says Babe with a laugh, "you're such a good old goose." She gives her sister's arm a squeeze and then she says, "Come on—we can't stay in here forever."

They push through the door, snap up their yellow umbrellas, kiss, and go their separate ways.

Fall 1898

Herbert Rowbarge sat on a bench in the Gaitsburg depot and drummed his fingers on the varnished oak armrest. It was hot for October, and though the stationmaster had propped open the depot's one door, there was no breeze at all to stir the fullness of cigar smoke and despair that hung in the long room. Herbert did not want to be inside, where the stationmaster, the flies, and the fat man on the bench opposite all seemed too much aware of him. But he didn't want to be outside, either, where a boy and a

girl about his own age were standing on the platform. It was better—no, not better, just not as bad—
to be stared at by the fat man than by the two holding
hands beside the tracks.

Herbert hated Gaitsburg. There was nothing about
his appearance to single him out as different, as A
Boy From The Home, but Gaitsburg still made him
feel he was wearing a sign that said, "Orphan Here,"
and that was the same thing as a sign that said,
"Nobody." The scowl that came so easily to his face
was there now and he shifted his weight restlessly.
It was all Dick's fault that he was sitting here. And
what would Dick be like when he got off the train?
All Herbert knew from the letter from Washington
was that Dick had been wounded at a place called
Daiquiri near Santiago, but that he would recover.
Recover! Good grief, what did *that* mean? Dick had
been three months in a hospital in Florida, and had
scrawled a dozen letters, but the letters were full of
longing for his wife and Herbert and the farm, and
said nothing about his physical condition except that
he was "getting better." Finally he had written to say
they were sending him home; he would arrive on
Tuesday, the 7th, or Wednesday.

It was Wednesday now, Wednesday afternoon.
Herbert had come to Gaitsburg five times to meet
trains, and Dick had not been on any of them. This
one would be the sixth, and it was late, just like all
the others. Herbert's scowl deepened. It was all so
dumb. Dumb and unnecessary.

Dick Festeen had gone back to his family's farm, and had worked even harder than he'd promised he would. He fixed the leaks in the farmhouse roof, cleared the mess from a field left fallow for years, and planted it to oats and potatoes. All this he accomplished on the very small savings his father had left behind at the Ohio Valley Bank in Gaitsburg. Things had been looking pretty good for Dick, and best of all he fell in love with Lollie Arbogast, a girl he'd known in grammar school, and married her in '97.

Then, in April of '98, just two months before Herbert's eighteenth birthday, Dick came to see him, on his regular weekly visit, all agog. "Bertie," he announced, "I'm joinin' up."

"Joinin' up what?" asked Herbert. They were of a height now, and could look each other in the eye, though Dick, at twenty-five, was still far thicker.

"Why, there's a war down in Cuba and a fella over to Portsmouth's raisin' a regiment! Didn't you hear about it?"

"Nope," said Herbert. They'd been standing on the steps of the veranda, and now Herbert sat down and stretched his long legs out to the weak spring sun. "We don't hear nothin' in this place. You know that."

"Well, anyway," said Dick, sitting down beside him, "I'm goin'. I can't hardly believe you didn't know about it. They sunk a big ship of ours down there. The *Maine*."

"Who did?" asked Herbert.

"Why, Spain, Bertie! Spain!"

"Oh," said Herbert. He'd heard of Spain, and he'd heard of Cuba, but they weren't real places to him, and the notion of going off to war about them seemed silly. "What you gonna do with Lollie?" The notion of Dick with a wife was almost as silly as the notion of Spain and Cuba, but Herbert had had longer to get used to it. He had been allowed to go to the wedding, and though he didn't think much of Lollie Arbogast, still, there hadn't been a thing he could do about her. Dick was smitten, and that was that.

"Well, look, Bertie, here's what I was thinkin'," said Dick, leaning toward him earnestly. "You'll be gettin' out in a coupla months, and I sure wish I was gonna be here for *that* day, you know that, but I'll be in the army, and . . . well, I was hopin' you'd go out to the farm and be with Lollie while I'm gone. I mean, that was what we was gonna do anyway, you comin' to the farm and all, and in case you think just because I'm away you shouldn't do it for some reason, I wanted to tell you the plan ain't changed. That farm's half yours as long as I got breath in my body, and all yours after that, and I'd sure feel better if I knowed you was out there with Lollie while I'm gone."

"Sure, I guess so," said Herbert warily. "I got nothin' else to do, anyway. You want me to sort of take care of Lollie for you?"

"Well, yeah, Bertie," said Dick, stroking his wide

jaw thoughtfully. "She don't want to go home to her mother, but she don't want to wait it out alone, either. She ain't too happy about me leavin'. But you're her brother-in-law, and I figure it'll be okay if you're there with her."

It had not been okay. For Lollie turned out to be pregnant and was sick almost all the time. Now, in October, she was in her seventh month and was having trouble getting about, for her legs and feet were swollen up like sausages. Herbert had to do everything, and though Lollie was a good sport and didn't complain, still, her dull eyes, ringed with violet circles, looked so unhappy that Herbert could scarcely bear to look at her. He did not like sickness.

And he did not like Lollie's mother, Mrs. Arbogast, either, a stringy, faded woman who was moved to tears by good and ill alike. She wept with equal feeling for Dick's heroism in joining up, and for his heartless abandonment of Lollie. She wept for the joy of Lollie's approaching motherhood and for the misery of her "women's problems." And she wept for Herbert's orphaning, and his obvious hatred of her pity. Her floods were as predictable as the river's, and tried Herbert's patience, which was slim at best, to the utmost. True, she brought fresh pies, and whole roasted chickens and hams, to the farm every week, and helped with the wash and the cleaning. Without her, and without the assistance of Mr. Arbogast while Dick was off in Cuba, the farm would have foundered and leaned once more toward decay.

Herbert knew all this, but he disliked Mrs. Arbogast anyway.

He disliked the farm even more: the ceaseless demands of the oats and potatoes, the brainless chickens with their fussy footwork and beady-eyed mistrust of him, the unshakable calm of the cow. He burned to get away. But he had promised Dick, and so had had to comfort himself with planning what they would do as soon as Dick returned. Now, however, Dick had been wounded and there was no telling what that might mean. Herbert shifted again on the hard bench. He could almost feel ropes tightening around him, stifling him, holding him forever to Gaitsburg and the farm.

The thin frame building began, almost imperceptibly, to tremble, and from far down the tracks came a high, faint shriek. The stationmaster sprang out from his cubicle and checked his pocket watch against the big round clock above the door. "Here she comes!" he cried to Herbert and the fat man. He settled his cap more firmly on his head and blew his nose, a nose so large and pocked and red, with nostrils so cavernous, that Herbert turned his eyes away quickly. But the stationmaster didn't notice. His cheeks were bright with pleasure. "Some dandy sight," he crowed. "Every durned time!" And he hurried outside to the platform.

Herbert stood up and followed as far as the doorway. The so-called romance of the rails was in no way romance to him, and he leaned unimpressed against the doorframe as the great iron monster

rolled bellowing toward him down the track, snort-
ing steam and gritty black cyclones of smoke. "Thar
she blows," yelled the fat man cheerfully. " 'Scuse
me, sonny, I got to get by." Herbert moved to let the
fat man out and leaned again, closing his eyes
against the grind and screech and the blasts of air
as the engine shivered to a halt. From a single coach,
hooked in among the boxcars, a conductor swung
down importantly and set a footstool on the platform
just under the metal steps. Herbert leaned and
watched. Maybe this time. He'd better be on it this
time.

A woman with a child climbed down, the conductor gallantly assisting. A drummer with straw
hat and sample case. A man in a uniform, a one-
legged man, with whom the conductor was solicitous
and gentle. Another drummer with . . . but wait. The
one-legged man in the uniform, hunching up the
platform on a crutch—he had taken off his hat and
was waving it at Herbert. His face was tight and
pale, but the bulk of the body, the sheaf of yellow
hair, were unmistakable. "Bertie!" cried the one-
legged man. "Bertie—thank God!"

It was Dick.

"But how're we gonna manage, Dick, with you all
busted up? Good lord, I'm no good at farming! I just
don't see how we're gonna manage!" Despair clogged
Herbert's throat, and he turned away to pace the
little kitchen.

Dick sat with Lollie at the table, exhaustion, pain, and joy keeping his gray eyes wet. "We'll manage fine," he said for the tenth time, with stolid, sweet confidence. "You're just tired, Bertie, after all the responsibility. You'll see—when the baby comes, Lollie'll feel much better, won't you, honey? And we'll all pitch in and make this the best ol' farm in the valley!"

But Herbert flung the back door open and rushed out into the cool October dark to stand alone, quivering, by the chicken yard. His first thought, at the depot, had been, "Now he'll be willing to let the farm go. How can a man with one leg be a farmer?" But now, *now*, it was plain that Dick loved the farm more than ever—and that Herbert would have to stay, could not even go away alone and leave him to it. There were his plans, he had his plans! Dick must be made to see. But not tonight. Not for a little while yet. It had better be soon, though. He clutched the rumpled chicken wire and wondered how long he could wait.

Deep into January, with a thin gauze of snow snagged across the stiff brown stubble of the fields, Lollie's baby was born. Dick held the bundled infant to his heart and whispered, "Frank. We'll call him Frank, honey. All right? After my brother that was drowned." And Lollie nodded weakly from the tumbled bed.

But she did not "feel much better," not at all. The

labor had been long and brutal, some fragile inner web had given way. Infection flared, spread wide, took over. In five days she was dead.

And in the spring a dazed and vulnerable Dick gave in at last. They would sell the farm. He and Herbert and Frank would sell the farm—and buy a merry-go-round.

But they did not sell the farm at once. For Herbert, eager as he was to be off and away, wanted to "do it right," as he said to Dick. "First we'll get the place in the best shape we can. That way it'll bring more money. And I got to find out all I can about what's the best merry-go-round to buy." Now that things were going his way, he was brisk, sure, efficient. He had taken charge.

He began to read the newspapers, that summer of '99, ignoring the Boer War and other far-off things that didn't matter, in favor of goings-on at home with regard to various kinds of machines. And off and on he traveled, when the money, and his presence, could be spared—walking, hitching rides on wagons, taking trains only when he had to. He went to Philadelphia, to the G. A. Dentzel Steam & Horsepower Caroussell Company; to Troy, to the Babcock plant; to Buffalo to see the Armitage Herschall factory. He even went to Kansas, where a man named Parker was making a portable machine called a carry-us-all. And at last he decided on Armitage Herschall. "They're the closest," he explained to Dick, "and in most ways the best."

But there seemed to be more to it than finding the best machine. "Look here, Dick," said Herbert. "It's just a question of time before they get 'em runnin' electric, like these new electric buggies they got comin' on so fast. They'll be better that way, and cleaner. And I been reading up on some of these parks they got. There's Coney Island, and another place out East called Prospect Park, and over to New Jersey they got one they call the Music Circus. Looks to me like it's better to pick one place, the way they're doin', where we can settle down, put up our machine, go electric when the time comes, and let the people come to us."

Dick brightened. "Say, that'd be all right! We could even do it here—we already got the land."

"Gaitsburg? Why'd anyone want to come to *this* jerkwater town?"

"Well," said Dick, chastened, "I don't know, Bertie, but it'd be easy enough, comin' by the river and all."

"Listen, Dick, nobody's comin' by the river any more. This place is the end of the world. You never been anywhere—you don't know what some of these other parts is like."

Dick had been to Cuba, but that, apparently, was not the same thing.

"Anyway," Herbert went on with ill-concealed impatience, "we got to sell *this* piece of land before we can buy the machine and some *other* piece of land. You know that. We been over it fifty times."

"Oh—well—yeah, that's right," said Dick. But he was sorrowful, and sometimes wondered how he had come to agree to anything so drastic. It had happened almost without his knowing it, and a lot of the time he felt confused. Selling the farm was like selling a piece of his heart. Still, Herbert claimed the largest piece of that heart. He always would. And Dick couldn't help admiring Herbert's grasp of it all, all the difficult details.

"I expect," said Herbert expansively, "we can find us a spot right here in Ohio."

This much, at least, was a relief. To go out of state—well, that would be so foreign. West Virginia was only a mile away, across the river. But it was full of West Virginians. And Dick had had enough of foreigners in Cuba.

Herbert made one more trip, in the fall of 1900. He had picked out a possible location with the help of a pile of maps, and now he needed to see it in the flesh. He came back thoroughly satisfied. "Red Man Lake, that's our place," he said to Dick. "Right up near the highest point in the state. They got a bunch of caves up there already that people come a long ways to see."

"Umm," said Dick. He was sitting with little Frank on his knee, playing peekaboo with a napkin, but it was clear that he was heavyhearted.

"What's the matter?" Herbert demanded.

With Herbert gone upstate, Dick had again lost sight of his shaky conviction that what they were about to do was right. "Well, Bertie," he said now, resting his chin forlornly on Frank's warm, tousled head, "I just been thinkin'. I mean, how'll it be for Frank? I got to start thinkin' about Frank. Why, he's almost two years old! A farm is a lot more secure, somehow, isn't it? You know, somethin' to leave him when I die."

"First place," said Herbert smoothly, knowing the battle was long since won, "first place, Dick, you're not gonna die. They got no floods upstate gonna carry you off like you lost your own folks. Second place, you can't do nothin' on a farm when you only got one leg. Third place, we're gonna make us a big pile of money up there, Dick. A big pile. Why, shoot, Frank can even go to college when he grows up, if you want him to."

"College?"

"Sure, college. Why not? And he can have a pony, and a big house to live in, and hold his head up anywhere he goes."

Dick nodded slowly. Herbert always made it sound so good—as if he, Dick, would be cheating Frank, somehow, if now he should back away. "Yeah, well," he sighed at last, "I guess you're right."

"Course I'm right," said Herbert kindly. And then he delivered the coup de grace: "You can take him for some real fishin', too, up on the lake. You can't do that here, on the river, not with one leg and the bottom all slippery. But up there, Dick, they got rowboats. Good fishin' out of rowboats, just sittin' down, all easy, right out in the middle of the lake."

They sold the farm the following spring, changing its twenty acres and its house and barn, plus cow, ten chickens, and a rooster, for three acres on the banks of Red Man Lake, in a little town called Mussel Point—three acres of lake-front land, and for one thousand dollars, a twelve-horse merry-go-round.

Sunday, May 25, 1952

Babe and Louisa Rowbarge have been to Sunday services this morning without Aunt Opal—her cold has turned out to be genuine—and now they walk away from the Lake Presbyterian Church in a thoughtful mood. Dr. Bray, the minister, has delivered himself of a throbbing harangue on the subject of honoring thy father and mother, and in spite of the fact that Babe and Louisa know, like everyone else in the congregation, that his wrath has been largely fueled by his son, Carmichael Bray, known fondly by high-school classmates as "Donkey," who the night before reeled home to the parsonage at 3 a.m. mellow and smelling of the cork, as the saying goes, though the Junior Prom had officially closed at eleven—Carmichael has long been a difficulty and in fact sat this morning in a front pew, looking more deaf than remorseful—in spite of the fact that Babe and Louisa know all this, still it's hard not to take a sermon personally.

"We always do the best we can for Daddy," says Louisa defensively, as they move down the sun-splotched sidewalk.

"And would've for Mother if we could've," Babe adds.

"We've never done *anything* bad," says Louisa.

"No, but he wasn't talking about *us*, necessarily," Babe reminds her.

"I know, but still," says Louisa. "I always come out of church feeling guilty. Do you think that's how we're meant to feel?"

"I don't know," says Babe. "Probably."

Louisa frowns and says, "The thing is, I try to honor Daddy, I really do, but he does make me mad sometimes, the way he won't try to tell us apart, even now, and . . . well, *you* know."

"I know," says Babe.

"But then I remember how old he's getting," Louisa goes on, "and I feel just terrible. I know I ought to be more patient."

"I don't see how you *could* be more patient," says Babe, "or me, either. It's not as if we yelled at him or slammed doors or anything."

They have reached by now the place on the street where the Rowbarge Lincoln and the Loose Olds-mobile stand grill to trunk, baking their chrome serenely in the sunshine. The insides of both—both sets of wool upholstery—look stuffy with accumulated heat, and rather than submit to being baked themselves, the twins open up a door apiece to let a small breeze in while they stand on the grassy curb and think about their father.

"Anyway," says Babe, "he's not so old. Look at Mr. Festeen—almost eighty! He's out of the hospital, by the way. It turned out to be nothing after all."

"That's good," says Louisa. "I hope he'll stay all right till Joe and Tammie's wedding." There is silence between them for a moment, and then Louisa says, "Sometimes in church I think about *them* getting married there. Mother and Daddy, I mean."

"I know," says Babe. "Me, too. I can just see them standing on the steps afterwards, like that picture Aunt Opal's got on the piano."

"Yes, I love that picture," says Louisa. "Mother looks so happy. And Daddy looks—well, now that I come to think of it, Daddy just looks like Daddy."

"He hasn't changed very much," says Babe.

"No," says Louisa.

"So that's what I mean," says Babe. "You talk about him like he had one foot in the grave or something. Why, he could easily live . . . oh, another twenty years, I suppose."

This observation sends them both into a second silence from which they are roused by a bee who has strayed into the Oldsmobile.

"Oh, now, look at that," says Babe. "We'd better get him out."

She hurries around to the driver's side and opens

the door, and she from that side and Louisa from the other, both bobbing, ducking, and squealing, flap awkwardly at the bee with their pocketbooks. The bee, all grace and danger, buzzes lazy figure eights near the ceiling, settles, and strolls calmly at the base of the windshield, ignoring them.

"Blast!" says Babe. "Now what?"

From the sidewalk a melodious voice asks, "Having a problem, ladies?" It is Dr. Bray. He is a heavy man with a barrel chest and large red hands who is playing in life the role of a pale, narrow man with small white hands. In the pulpit it's rather effective, for his passion is intense. But out of the pulpit he tends to vacillate, so that public opinion sometimes sways toward him, and sometimes toward his erring son, Carmichael.

"Oh, good morning, Dr. Bray," says Babe. "There's a bee in my car."

"Ah!" he says. "And you're afraid of bees."

"Well," says Louisa, "they sting!"

Dr. Bray steps to the curb and leans into the Oldsmobile. "Like most of us," he says, his voice somewhat muffled, "they only sting when they're attacked." The bee has resumed its figure eights, and Dr. Bray, straightening up, says, "We'll have to wait until it lands somewhere. Tell me—where was Mrs. Loose this morning? Not ill, I hope?"

"She's got a cold," says Babe. "She'll be all right."

"I'm relieved to hear it," he says. "Now if we could just bring your dear father into the flock!"

Louisa, embarrassed, says, "Oh, well."

The bee makes a landing on the dashboard and Dr. Bray leans in again. All at once he is not small and pale, but large and vengeful. With a swift, heavy movement, he brings a hard red palm down on the bee so forcefully that the car bounces.

"My goodness!" says Louisa.

The minister steps back, the dead bee between finger and thumb. "When you strike at a king, strike hard," he says with a gentle smile, and drops the bee into the gutter.

"Well . . . thank you," says Babe.

"*We* were just going to *shoo* him out," says Louisa faintly.

Dr. Bray does not hear the reproach in her voice. "I'm glad I was here to help," he says. "Good day, ladies."

When he's gone, Babe says, "I wonder if he beats up on Carmichael."

"Daddy never laid a *glove* on *us*," says Louisa. "Poor bee."

The congregation has dispersed by now and the street is hushed with Sunday. "I'd better get going," says Babe. "It's almost time for dinner."

But Louisa isn't ready to let her go. Not quite. "Babe," she says, leaning down to speak through the open door as, from the other side, her sister slides in under the wheel, "Babe, do you really think he'll live another twenty years?"

"Daddy?" says Babe. "He could."

"We'll be sixty-five by then," says Louisa wonderingly. "Old ourselves."

"We're not really young *now*," says Babe.

The bee forgotten, Louisa says, "I'm tired of living apart."

"I know, dear," says Babe. "Me, too."

Louisa straightens up, then leans once more into the Oldsmobile. "Babe," she says, "are you sorry we never got married?"

"Married? Certainly not! Who could ever love and understand us as much as *we* do?"

"That's what *I* always think," says Louisa gratefully. And then she says, her eyes suddenly alight, "Listen, Babe, this is the last Sunday before the park opens. Let's rent a rowboat this afternoon, if they don't need us for anything, and go for a row on the lake while it's still not crowded."

"That's a wonderful idea!" Babe exclaims.

"Oh, good. I'll pick you up. Let's wear our denim wrap skirt."

"All right," says Babe. "And the pink blouse. And a hat, too—it's a hot sun."

"Which hat?"

"Oh—the natural straw, I guess. No point in getting all dressy."

"All right," says Louisa. "Doesn't it sound like *fun*? Oh, Babe, I just love summer."

"Me, too," says Babe. "Me, too."

August 1903

Herbert Rowbarge stood in front of the bureau, brushing his hair. It was important to look as good as possible, because he was taking Ruby Nill for a Sunday row on the lake, and so he leaned forward impatiently, trying to see himself better. The mirror was in every way inadequate—far too small, its surface blotched, a very irritating mirror—and Herbert Rowbarge scowled.

"Whatcha doin' *now*, Uncle Bertie?" asked little Frank from the bed behind. Little Frank was sitting cross-legged, eating an applesauce sandwich, and his cheeks and smock were generously smeared.

"For goodness' sake, go eat that stuff somewhere else, can't you?" Herbert barked.

Frank chewed calmly, swallowed, and repeated, "Whatcha doin' *now*?"

"I'm brushing my *hair*." Herbert leaned forward again toward the mirror, with narrowed eyes. He wished little Frank would go away. He wished his hair would hold its center part. He wished . . . and then he paused. A twinkling sensation had skipped down his spine as he looked into the eyes of his reflection, and, brush in midair, he waited, frozen, to see if it would come again.

Every once in a while it happened, that twinkling sensation, when he saw himself in mirrors, and it always made him giddy and confused, and unable to decide whether the feeling was terrible or sweet. "I'm going crazy," he would think, fleetingly, and then the sensation would pass. So he stayed away from mirrors as much as he could, but you couldn't stay away altogether. This jacket, now, with its gay blue stripes—trying it on at the haberdasher's, he had stepped in front of a big double mirror at the back of the store and for the first time had seen himself, all six feet of him, standing there beside himself—a pair of Herberts, head to toe—and had had to turn away at once and walk about, trying to look casual, till the feeling went away. It had been very strong that day, so strong it frightened him. Still, it had been worth it. The jacket was exactly right. It had cost a lot, but you couldn't court a girl like Ruby Nill in rags and tatters. And anyway, they were making a fair amount of money, he and Dick, this second summer in Mussel Point, running the merry-go-round and the new shooting gallery. He could afford the jacket, and the straw hat waiting on a chair beside the bureau. He picked up the hat and put it on, tilting it at a rakish angle.

"Whatcha doin' *now?*" said little Frank.

"What's it *look* like I'm doing?" Herbert roared, exasperated. "I'm putting on my *hat.*"

"Why?" said Frank.

Herbert stalked out of the bedroom and went down

the hall to the parlor. This cottage—it was far too
small, just like the mirror. Three in one bedroom
was too much like the Home. Worse, even, since one
of the three was only four years old. Well, they would
be doing better soon. Soon he and Dick would each
have a house of their own, and his would not be anything like this. His would have an upstairs to it, and
an indoor bathroom. "Now, listen, Dick," he said,
"you got to get Frank off the bed. He's getting applesauce all over everything."

Dick put down the newspaper he'd been reading.
"Says here," he reported, "fellow went all the way
across the Irish Channel in a balloon."

"Balloon, eh?" said Herbert. "That's interesting.
Maybe we should get a balloon ride. We could run it
back and forth across the lake."

"Gee, I dunno, Bertie," said Dick, stretching out
his good leg with a comfortable sigh. "You already
got a list a mile long, things you want to get."

"That's right," said Herbert, "and I'm going to get
'em, too. All of 'em."

Dick shook his head at this, smiling, but as usual
he was full of admiration. And astonishment.

"How do I look?" asked Herbert, readjusting the
hat.

"Real nice," said Dick. "You goin' out to see Ruby?"

"Yep. Taking her rowing."

"Bertie," said Dick carefully, "how come you're
spending every Sunday on Ruby? You don't even
like her. Least, that's what you said before."

"Ruby's all right," said Herbert. "Any girl with a banker for a father's all right. And she's sweet on me."

"You better be careful you don't break her heart," said Dick, smiling again.

"I'm not going to break her heart," said Herbert. "I'm going to marry her."

Dick's smile faded. "Marry her? When you don't even like her?"

"Now, listen, Dick," said Herbert. "We got to get more money, don't we?"

"Nope," said Dick. "We're doing fine."

"Well, I say we got to get more money, and this is the best way to do it. Once I'm married to Ruby, we can get a loan from the bank any time we need it, and start to do things right." He sat down opposite Dick and took off the straw hat. "Look here," he said. "I'm going to marry Ruby whether you like it or not. She's no beauty, but she's what we need. And you got to help me."

"How?" said Dick, torn between shock and loyalty. "What can I do?"

"It's this way, Dick," said Herbert. "I don't want you blabbing about the Home and Gaitsburg and me being an orphan and all that. Ruby's father and that durned sister of hers'd never go for that. They're pretty high-toned people. I told Ruby I got money from an aunt I lived with after my folks died. So now she thinks I'm high-toned, too. And I don't want you saying anything different."

"But, Bertie, what's so bad about saying the money come from selling the farm? You don't know anything about your folks. Or an aunt or anybody."

"Well, I know that," Herbert exploded. "But Ruby doesn't have to know it. She thinks I come from good people down to Cincinnati, and I don't want you spoiling it. You got to promise me, Dick."

Dick took his crutch, rose, and swung to the window, where he stood silent for a moment. "I don't like telling lies, Bertie," he said at last. "I'd do anything for you, you know that, but I don't like telling lies."

"Listen, Dick. Now just listen," said Herbert patiently. "You're lucky. You *know* about your folks. But Mrs. Frate never told me anything about mine. Not one blamed word. So how do we know they *weren't* high-toned? They might as well have been. Isn't that right?"

"We-ell," said Dick.

"So," said Herbert, "it's not like telling lies if we don't know what the truth is, is it? Except for the aunt part. But who cares about aunts? If it makes old man Nill happy to think I had a rich aunt, what's the difference? What harm does it do? But I s'pose you think I don't look like I could've had a rich aunt," he added with a scowl. "I s'pose you think I look like some kind of goddamn gypsy."

"Course I don't, Bertie." Dick turned around to face him earnestly. "Anybody'd be proud to have you in their family."

Herbert's face cleared. "Well, then!" he said in triumph. "There you are. So promise you'll back me up."

"Well, all right, Bertie," said Dick reluctantly, wondering how he'd been maneuvered into yet another uncomfortable promise. Still, he had to admit Bertie did have a way about him, somehow. Maybe he *did* come from high-toned folks, after all. You couldn't tell. And he sure was smart. They were doing real well, just like he'd said they would. Course, it wasn't like having the farm, not at all, but, well, Bertie never had wanted the farm, and if he was happy . . .

Herbert put his hat back on and stood up. "Get Frank off the bed, will you? I'll be home in a couple of hours. Oh, and by the way, Dick," he added, all in a rush, "I told Ruby I'm a Kenyon man. Class of 1900."

"*Bertie! Gee whiz!*"

Herbert laughed. "She thinks it's swell," he said. "C'mon, Dick, don't be such a prig. I'm doing it all for us. For you and me and Frank. Remember, now, class of 1900." And he clapped Dick on the back and hurried out the door.

Herbert at twenty-three looked much as he had at seven—light brown hair, long nose, sharp eyes. The difference was that the sharpness became him more, now that he was grown, than it had when he was little. It made him look hard-driving. It made him look as if he knew what he was doing. Now, in the boat with Ruby Nill, he did know what he was doing, and he was doing it very well. Ruby gazed at him adoringly as he pulled on the oars, and then, catching herself, she turned her gaze away and looked back to the dock, where her younger sister, Opal, sat watching, like the narrow-eyed chaperone she'd been sent along to be.

"We mustn't stay out too long, Mr. Rowbarge," said Ruby primly, tucking her long skirts tight around her ankles. "Opal will want to get back soon."

"Opal, Opal, Opal," said Herbert. "How am I supposed to remember about Opal, or anything else, when I'm with you?" Ruby blushed, and Herbert, noting the blush, smiled to himself. He had practiced this kind of talk on girls at the Home, and had discovered he had a sort of knack for it.

Ruby tilted her parasol over one shoulder and trailed her fingers in the water, as she'd seen a girl do in a magazine picture. Ruby was twenty-two, and her father and sister had been afraid no one would ever marry her. It had been hard on Opal, who, at nineteen, had a serious suitor. A doctor, too, Dr. Stuart Loose, who'd been to the university and everything. But Father had felt that Opal should wait, that Ruby, as the eldest, should marry first. Still, Stuart Loose wouldn't hold on forever. And then, just when Ruby had begun to despair, this wonderful man had suddenly appeared, this beautiful, wonderful man who didn't seem to notice that she was a little too thick and short to look like a real Gibson Girl, or that her hair, no matter how she struggled, was a little too fly-away and thin to stay pinned obediently around its rat. He seemed to think she was . . . well . . . acceptable, anyway. At the very least, acceptable. Ruby looked out across the water and blushed again. They'd been together every Sunday for months now, and Ruby didn't want to understand it. She just wanted to believe in it. He really was wonderful—and a comer, too. Even her father said so.

"You look fine today, Miss Nill," said Herbert, keeping his voice low and soft. "But then, you always do."

"Oh, Mr. Rowbarge," she fluttered, "you mustn't say such things."

"Why mustn't I?" he demanded. "It's the truth!"

"Well . . ." she said, looking away.

"And you know it, too," he added. "You're such a tease. I think you're trying to break my heart."

"Oh, Mr. Rowbarge!" she murmured, charmed and aghast both at once. She—a tease? She would have loved to believe herself a tease, but hadn't realized she even knew how. Opal would laugh at her, as usual, when she reported this conversation. Opal didn't like Mr. Rowbarge.

"You're such a dummy, Ruby," Opal had said. "Don't you see? He only likes you because we're rich."

And she had answered, hotly, "That's not so, Opal. How can you be so mean? Why, he's got lots of money of his own!"

This did appear to be true, but Opal was not silenced. "And a merry-go-round! What kind of work is that?"

"I think it's romantic!" Ruby had said stoutly. "Romantic and lovely, to want to give people pleasure. He says he'll have a big park here someday, just like the ones out East."

"Well, go ahead and make a fool of yourself if you want to," Opal had said with a shrug. "But I don't trust him."

"You don't have to trust him," Ruby retorted in a rare show of spirit. "He isn't sweet on *you*."

"Thank goodness for that," Opal had snapped. "I wouldn't have him if he *was*."

But Mr. Rowbarge—Herbert—was far handsomer than Stuart Loose, and smarter, too. Ruby decided Opal was merely jealous—imagine! how satisfying! —and made up her mind to ignore her.

They slipped across the warm brown water smoothly, and soon, rounding a wooded little island, Herbert rested on the oars and let the rowboat drift. They were out of sight of the dock now, where Opal sat waiting, and here, in the shadow of willows leaning from the banks, the August air was cooler and smelled delicious. Herbert sniffed, half closing his eyes. His mood was rare and dreamy, as it always was out on the lake, for he had discovered that he loved to go rowing. There was something deeply soothing to this floating about in boats.

"Now, this is the stuff," he said, opening his eyes

again and looking at Ruby with meaning. "Just you and me. I wish it could always be this way."

Ruby caught her breath and tried to think of an answer, but nothing came. Why, it was almost a proposal, what he'd said! She wondered weakly if she ought to swoon. Would that be proper, or . . . of course, if she swooned, unless he was near enough to catch her, she might fall out of the boat and . . . no, dear me, she mustn't swoon! Trembling, she closed her parasol and laid it beside her on the wooden seat. Then: "I brought some poems to read," she gasped, holding up a little book. "I thought we could read some poems. And then I expect we'd better get back."

"Poems?" said Herbert. "Oh. All right. That would be nice."

"All right," said Ruby bravely. "I'll go first. It's Samuel Taylor Coleridge. Here's one"—opening the book. "It's called 'Kubla Khan.' "

"All right," said Herbert.

And Ruby began in a small, singsong voice:

> *In Xanadu did Kubla Khan*
> *A stately pleasure dome decree:*
> *Where Alph, the sacred river—*

"Wait a minute," said Herbert, sitting forward. "What does he say there?"

" 'Where Alph, the sacred river'?"

"No. Before that."

"Well, let me see. 'In Xanadu did Kubla Khan a stately pleasure dome—' "

"That's it!" Herbert exclaimed. " 'A stately pleasure dome.' Say, that's grand! By Jove, Miss Nill, that's what I'm going to call my park. The Pleasure Dome. The Rowbarge Pleasure Dome."

"Oh, Mr. Rowbarge," Ruby sighed, her eyes starry. "That would be beautiful!"

"It's going to be a dilly, Miss Nill," said Herbert. "I'm going to get a bigger merry-go-round pretty soon, a better one, and then one of these new rides they call a Ferris wheel. And after that—well, by the time I'm done, this town'll be famous all around the state."

"Oh, Mr. Rowbarge," Ruby sighed again. "You're just so smart! Even Father says so."

Herbert, fired by this last, seized the moment. "Miss Nill—Ruby—won't you share it with me? If you were with me, everything would be a pleasure, the whole dad-blasted world. Can I speak to your father now? Today? I can't wait any longer." In one quick movement he came forward to his knees and put his arms around her, marveling, himself, at his eloquence. And Ruby, conquered, dropped the book into the lake, where it bobbed off daintily a little way before it sank. She hadn't gotten to the part in the poem where the woman wails for her demon lover. But, oh, she would. She would.

Monday morning, May 26, 1952

The Loose house, since the start of Aunt Opal's widowhood, has slowly taken on a different cast. Gone is the doctor's old armchair with its crumb-dry sifting of pipe tobacco trapped forever in the crevasses beneath its cushion. Here instead, by the fireplace, stands a handsome wing chair upholstered in gold brocade. His study, where for years he hid from Opal and devoured the magazines he knew she disapproved of, is a card room now, with bright new carpeting and curtains that smell like the shops they came from, not like Stuart. The old things from this room have all been moved to Walter's apartment, and the stacks of magazines, too, whisked away by Walter before his mother had a chance to burn them. Gone is the portable bar, a walnut cabinet on wheels, with bottles and glasses in clever interior racks and a white tile top with the words *What'll You Have* embellished on it. Walter has taken this as well, though he has covered the top, which he says was "corny," with a cutting board for sandwiches, lemons, and limes. Walter leads an active social life.

Upstairs, the room that was Walter's in his boyhood is a second guest room now, done over in dusty rose, with new white-painted beds and bureau, and a dressing table skirted in white eyelet to match the curtains. This room, like the rest of the house, is not so much feminized as ordered. There is no "man's mess" anywhere.

Babe stands at the white-painted bureau brushing her hair, for it is this room she shares, on an alternating basis, with Louisa. For five years it has been constantly occupied by one or the other, but it shows no signs of wear or the softening that some rooms—some houses—acquire from long habitation by a loving owner. That softening, in fact, is what Aunt Opal especially dislikes. Except for a few framed photographs, the house, from cellar to attic, could belong to anyone—or no one. It is dust-free, scratch-free, flawless as a scalpel, and living there is like living in a fine, and very new, hotel. It was hard to keep the house this way while Stuart and Walter were in it. But now Aunt Opal can walk through the rooms and feel a pleasure so rich that sometimes she is nearly moved to tears. Aunt Opal isn't glad that Stuart's gone, but still, she's not entirely sorry, either.

Her nieces have placed on the white-painted bureau three photographs of their own: one of themselves arm in arm on the day of their high-school graduation; one of their father, a formal portrait taken some years back and retouched to vacuity, a state quite unlike him, by a zealous Bell Fountain photographer; and one, an enlarged snapshot, of their mother standing in bright sunlight beside a wicker double stroller on the seat of which they, at the age of one, sag dangerously, bonnets askew, staring blankly at infinity. The picture is fuzzy, but their mother's expression is clear: she looks astonished.

Aunt Opal has said that their mother often looked that way. "She had two expressions," Opal told them once. "Surprised, like that"—indicating the snapshot—"and asleep."

Hurt, they said, "Didn't you like her?"

And she said, surprised, now, herself, "Of *course* I did. She was my sister! What a question."

It was a question they did not raise again.

Babe puts down the hairbrush and rubs her shoulders. She is stiff from her turn at the oars on the lake the day before. But the afternoon in the rowboat was a great success. She and Louisa have decided to do it again some afternoon this week, and Babe is just wondering whether she ought to call Louisa and set a date, when the phone on the bedside table rings.

"I'll get it," she calls to Aunt Opal, who is dressing in her own room down the hall. She picks up the receiver and says, "Hello?"

It's Louisa. Breathlessly she says, "Babe? Listen, I've only got a minute. Walter and I are taking Daddy to a doctor over in Bell Fountain this morning. In just a few minutes, as soon as Walter gets here. But I wanted to call and let you know."

Babe sits down suddenly on the bed and says, "Louisa—what's wrong?"

"Well," says her sister with a quaver, "I'm not really sure. He had a sort of spell at breakfast. He seemed to forget where he was. And he looked at me and he said in this funny, really loud sort of voice, 'What?'"

"'What?'" Babe echoes.

"Yes. What. And I hadn't said *anything*."

"Oh, dear," says Babe.

"And then," says Louisa, "oh, Babe, he tried to stand up and he couldn't. His legs just buckled under him."

"Louisa—how terrible—what did you *do*?"

"Well," says Louisa, "I didn't do anything right off. I guess I just sat there. And then—then—he was all *right* again."

Babe has pressed her fingers to her lips. She feels, all at once, very cold.

"Babe?" says Louisa anxiously. "Are you still there?"

"I'm here," says Babe. "I'm just . . . trying to figure it out. So did you call Dr. Herdman?"

"Yes," says Louisa. "I got up and didn't say what I was doing, and I went and called him, but I couldn't reach him. His daughter . . . Helen?"

"Ellen," says Babe.

"Well, anyway, she graduated from college yesterday and he went over for it and won't be back till tomorrow. So I didn't know *what* to do, so I called Walter and he knows this doctor over in Bell Fountain at the clinic—at least, he knows his nurse . . ."

"Of course he'd know the *nurse*," says Babe.

"And so he said he'd make an appointment and be right down to help me talk Daddy into going."

"Louisa," says Babe, standing up, "I'd better come over."

"Oh—no, Babe, there isn't time. Walter will be here any . . . he's here now, Babe, he's coming up the driveway."

"All right," says Babe. "Now, look—you go along and don't worry about me. I'll call the clinic myself in a couple of hours and see what's what. Which doctor is it?"

"Marks."

"All right," says Babe. "Chin up. I'll talk to you later."

Louisa hangs up and Babe stands by the phone for a moment. She feels heavy, her insides feel heavy, and tired. Poor Daddy, she thinks. Then she puts the receiver back in its cradle and wanders over to the bureau.

"Who was it?" calls Aunt Opal from down the hall.

"Louisa," Babe answers.

"It beats me," says Aunt Opal, "how you two can find so much to talk about all hours of the day."

Babe feels too heavy just now to explain. She picks up the hairbrush again, and holds it in her hand, and stares at the picture of her mother. "He can't be really sick," she thinks. "Not Daddy. People like Daddy go on forever." But she knows, even before the thought has passed, that this is nonsense. It's just that it seems—too soon. She lays the brush down carefully and says to the astonished woman in the photograph, "I guess life *is* full of surprises."

September 1907

There are plenty of reasons for a man's getting married that don't have anything to do with love. After all, human needs quite often go beyond the willing ear in the evening, the soft arms in the night. Herbert Rowbarge had felt a human need for the warm hand in the wallet, and in this he was by no means the first. Nevertheless, he thought it probable that marriage would demand of him at least some loverlike behavior, and so, before his wedding, he went to Dick for the facts to flesh out—fortunate phrase!— what little he had learned about girls from those rare glimpses at the Home which had so far served him as his only solid instruction on the female anatomy. But Dick, crimson with embarrassment, was unable to tell him much. "Don't worry about it, Bertie" was all he could manage. "You'll know how to do it when the time comes."

And of course he had. The opulent Cleveland hotel

room with its oceanic bed, the bottle of wine at supper, Ruby's ample breasts—the authenticity of these
last long a subject of speculation on Herbert's part
after all those pictures of ruffle-padded corsets in
catalogues—all these served to cool his apprehension
and heat his purpose. And Ruby, terrified at first, had
suddenly, well into the process, seized him round
the hips with her two hands and guided him blindly
but confidently home. Afterward she had wept with
shame at her own shuddering pleasure—it was not
supposed to be that way at all!—and the sight of
her streaming nose and eyes above the rumpled mess
of her nightdress deflated any urge he might have
had to go another round. Still, it was done, and he
felt relieved and only faintly disgusted.

What did disgust him, finally, over the three years
following, was Ruby's enthusiasm for the thing.
From everything he had read—which wasn't much
but was certainly unanimous—men were the ones
who wanted these bedtime scuffles, not women. But
with Ruby and him it was just the opposite, and soon
he came to dislike her for it. Let them only close the
door to their bedroom—in the fine little house old
man Nill had bought for them—and there was Ruby
mooning at him in that moist, annoying way, word-
less but hopeful, that robbed him entirely of what
was at best only a thin desire. Why, Ruby was *easy*!
It would have been shocking in any case, but in so
unattractive a girl, it was also somehow repellent.
Nine times out of ten he would turn away and leave
her to sigh alone on her own side of the bed.

So when, in February of 1907, she proved to be pregnant, he was glad. Lovemaking, the doctor had assured her, would be dangerous now. Herbert must be made to cool his passion—and his heels—in the second bedroom till long after the baby was born. The doctor—his brother-in-law, Stuart Loose—was firm about this, and had had a little talk with Herbert on the subject. "At times like these, Herbert," he said ponderously, "we must put mother and child above all other considerations."

Herbert, more than willing to do so, said, "Certainly, Stuart. Certainly."

There were times when Stuart allowed what he believed was a flash of the manly rakehell to leer through his medical reserve. He allowed it to leer through now. Jabbing Herbert in the ribs, he roared, "No cheating, now, you rascal! Leave the poor girl alone."

Herbert had fled to the Pleasure Dome as soon as this interview was over, and there he stood for a long time in the cold, crisp air, gazing at his new merry-go-round. This one was complete with twenty pairs of animals, and only half were horses. There was, at last, a pair of lions, poised forever side by side in a graceful forward leap, and he put out a hand to caress their varnished manes. How proud they were! He was eased here of all his irritations, even when, as now, the park was closed for the season. Especially, perhaps, when it was closed. Nearby, in the shooting gallery, Dick was cleaning the long row of guns, for Dick had taken over maintenance at the park. He liked caring for things, he said, and was pleased with his title of General Manager. Herbert strolled over to where he was working. "Stuart says I got to stay away from Ruby till the baby comes," he reported happily.

"Yes, they say that's the safest thing," said Dick. "Never mind, Bertie. It'll be over soon."

"But I *don't* mind," said Herbert. "Not in the least."

Dick put down his rag and can of oil and leaned across the gallery counter to touch this strange little brother. "Bertie," he said wonderingly, "don't you care for her at all?"

But Herbert turned away and went again to gaze at the merry-go-round. The lions were exactly alike in every particular. He had ordered them that way on purpose. It was what he had always wanted, and he was deeply satisfied.

And then, on a wet September day, with remarkably little trouble, Herbert became a father. There was not much to it, none of the fuss he'd feared, for Ruby's labor was nothing compared to that of Lollie Festeen. Resolutely repressing memories of that other confinement, Dick was there to stand by him, and Opal was there to stand by Ruby, and old man Nill came, too. They waited, all of them, in the parlor, while upstairs Stuart Loose and Ruby moved through the ancient rite with hardly any racket. And a little after four o'clock Stuart came down the stairs, beaming. "Herbert, old man," he boomed, "bully for you! You've got a first-rate set of twins! Girls, and beauties, and Ruby's fine. Go on up and congratulate her."

At once there was tumult in the parlor, but Herbert went up the stairway in a daze. In the bedroom he stood dumfounded, staring at Ruby and the two snug bundles tucked one in the crook of each elbow.

"Oh, Herbert," Ruby whispered, as happy tears slid down across her cheeks. "Isn't it just wonderful! Come and look at them, the darlings."

He went nearer, and looked. They were, like the lions, exactly alike. But deep in the pit of his stomach he felt a dull resentment. It was just like Ruby to do this to him. Do this? Do what? He didn't know, but he didn't like it. Not at all. Twins! He stared at them, and the dull resentment swelled, tightening his throat. "Yes," he mumbled, "it's certainly grand."

"Oh, Herbert, what shall we call them? How about May and June? Or—let's see—Phoebe and Hebe?"

"Good grief, no," he said with a scowl. "I hate trick names."

"Well," said Ruby, taken aback by his tone, "then, maybe, dear, how about if I name one, and you name the other? Would you like that?"

"I suppose so," said Herbert. "All right."

"Then I think I'll choose Louisa," said Ruby. "Louisa May Rowbarge." She'd been reading *Little Women* all summer. "What would you like to choose?"

But Herbert could come up with nothing. He couldn't seem to put his mind to the task. For weeks the twins were known as Baby and Louisa. And finally everyone was so used to it that when the christening day arrived, they made it permanent, with only one small change, and Babe and Louisa Rowbarge were formally anointed and licensed to begin their own long passage out, around, and back.

Three years later, in the spring of 1910, Opal and Stuart Loose had a baby of their own, and named him Walter. A boy, and only *one*. Now, that, said Herbert to himself, was sensible. He gave the infant a brand-new Noah's Ark, and began to think more kindly of Opal.

Monday forenoon, May 26, 1952

Babe turns Aunt Opal's Oldsmobile into the driveway of her father's house and even now, when she is baffled and anxious, she thinks what a nice house it is. Far and away the nicest house in Mussel Point, or Bell Fountain, as nice as any she has seen in Lima or Cleveland. Not a mansion, maybe—and thank goodness for *that*—it was hard enough for her and Louisa always to be the richest girls all the way through school—but still imposing. Brick painted white, green shutters, light post, birdbath, a playhouse out back when she and Louisa were children, everything. Well, she thinks for the thousandth time, Daddy was used to the best in Cincinnati; it's nice he can afford the best in Mussel Point.

She leaves the car in the turnaround, goes through the open garage, where her father's Lincoln drowses in the oily cool, and with a quick knock lets herself into the kitchen. The "girl"—meaning the woman who comes in daily to clean and cook supper—turns from the sink and says, "Hiya." Her name is Fawn and she is one of a long succession of "girls"—all of them middle-aged—who have graced the Rowbarge house in the last twenty years. Before that, there were always two, but with Babe and Louisa grown, that came to seem excessive, as indeed it was. They have, since then, done all the light cleaning themselves. They like to. And anyway, there isn't much of it to do.

"Oh, hello, Fawn," says Babe. "Where's Louisa?"

"I dunno," says Fawn. "Somewheres around. Upstairs, maybe. She was trompin' around up there when I come in."

Babe says, "Where's my father?"

Fawn turns back to the sink. "Gone," she says.

The word has a flat, final sound. Oh, God, Babe thinks. She hurries down the hall to the front of the house and calls, "Louisa? *Louisa!*"

"Is that you, Babe?" Louisa answers, and in a moment she is fluttering down the stairs. "Babe, I've been calling and calling, but your line was busy."

"I was trying to call *you*," says Babe. "What happened? I rang up Dr. Marks, but the nurse said you'd cancelled the appointment."

Louisa says, "Oh, Babe, what a morning! I'm a wreck. Want some coffee?"

"Coffee!" Babe exclaims. "Louisa, for heaven's sake, where's Daddy? What happened?"

"He refused to go," says Louisa. "Even Walter couldn't budge him."

"But—" Babe begins.

"No, no, it's all right," Louisa reassures her. "He's really all right. Come on, let's get some coffee. There's lots left over from breakfast."

They go back to the kitchen and find that Fawn has set a sudsy bucket in the doorway. "You can't come in here now," she says. "I got to mop."

"We just want to get a cup of coffee," Louisa explains. "We won't get in your way."

"*Not now,*" says Fawn.

"But, Fawn," says Babe, "you haven't even started yet!"

Fawn is accustomed to command. Though not yet fifty-five, she is the mother of six and the grandmother of ten, and all are mortally afraid of her. "See this?" she says, brandishing the mop. "See that?"—pointing to the bucket. "That says work. You two'll come out here and you'll fiddle around and spill the sugar and use up more dishes when I just got 'em done up from breakfast, and all the time the bucket's gettin' cold and I'm standin' here gettin' older every minute. *No,* sir. No coffee. Too much coffee gives you the gripes anyhow, didn't you know that?"

Babe and Louisa are *not* accustomed to command. "Oh, well," says Louisa nervously, "never mind."

"Never mind is right," says Fawn, and she plunges the mop into the bucket.

The twins retreat to the living room and sit down side by side on the sofa.

"So, anyway," says Babe, "what happened?"

"Well," says Louisa, "Walter came over—but you know that already—and Daddy said, 'Just the man I wanted to see, let's go down to the park, I want to check the'—whatever it was, I don't remember—and Walter said, 'Now wait a minute, Uncle Herbert, Louisa says you're not feeling well,' and Daddy said he'd be the judge of that and what did *I* know; if I was referring to his falling asleep at the breakfast table, *that* didn't mean anything, he just hadn't slept well last night because he was worried about the— that thing he wanted to check on at the park."

Babe, heartened, says, "Well—maybe that's really all it was. Do you think so?"

"*I* don't know," says Louisa. "Maybe. He certainly *seemed* all right by then. His color was good, and all that. So then Walter said it might be a good idea for him to let a doctor look him over, and *Daddy* said he'd be damned if he'd turn himself over to any idiot doctor."

Babe smiles at this.

"I know," says Louisa. "Daddy said, 'Excuse me, Walter, I don't mean to cast aspersions on your father's memory,' and Walter said, 'Think nothing of it, Uncle Herbert. Father *was* an idiot!' And of course Daddy loved that. He laughed and laughed."

"Good grief," says Babe, laughing, herself. "Isn't Walter terrible!"

"Of course he is," says Louisa. "That's why Daddy likes him so much."

Babe settles back limply on the cushions and says,

"Well, I was prepared for everything to be all hay-wire, and now that it's not, I don't know *what* to do. Where *is* Daddy?"

"Down at the park, of course," says Louisa. "He went down with Walter. I remember now what he wanted to look at. Something to do with the Tunnel of Love, something minor like a stiff lever or some-thing. Babe, I guess he really is all right. I mean, what could be serious that could come and *go* like that? After he said that, about going to sleep at the table, it did seem to me that's probably what it was. So, *I* don't know. I feel like the boy who cried wolf. I'm really sorry to get you so upset."

"Never mind," says Babe. "After all, we're not doctors. And anyway, he never used to go to sleep at the table. I'd have done just what you did."

"He never used to be seventy-two, either, though," says Louisa. "I think when Dr. Herdman gets back I'll call and tell him what's been going on. You know. Just to make sure. Because he did have that other little spell last week—remember? When I said he got dizzy? So it wouldn't hurt just to check it out."

"No," says Babe. "That's a good idea. Well. Whew! I'm really relieved. I really thought there for a while . . ."

"So did I," says Louisa. "And it scared me silly."

"You know," says Babe, "they say when your mother dies you've gone through the worst there is. But I don't remember anything about that. Do you?"

"Not much," says Louisa. "A little bit about the

funeral, I think, but that's all. But we were so *little*, Babe. And we already had that nurse—remember her?—so I don't suppose it was much of an up-heaval or anything." And then she smiles and adds, "It's kind of sweet Daddy never married again."

"Well, he had us," says Babe. "Maybe if he hadn't already had *us*, he would have."

"Maybe," says Louisa. "But sometimes I think he married the park instead."

From the kitchen comes the clank of the bucket and a rush and gurgle as Fawn dumps water into the sink. Then she comes down the hall and stands in the archway, hands on hips. "I got to vacuum," she says.

"All right," says Louisa.

Fawn stares at them in silence for a moment and then she says, "Well?"

"Well what?" says Babe.

"Well, clear out!" says Fawn. "I got to *vacuum*. And stay outa the kitchen. The floor ain't dry."

"Oh, dear," says Louisa. "Well, come on upstairs, Babe, and tell me if you think the present looks all right."

They stand up, and Babe says, "No, I probably better go. Aunt Opal needs the car."

"Use the front," says Fawn as they pass, "so's you don't track up the kitchen."

Louisa walks out with Babe to the driveway. "Fawn's so bossy," she says. "I suppose I ought to stand up to her, but I'm afraid to. She might quit or something, or bawl me out."

"I know," says Babe. "She *is* kind of big. I forget when I'm not around her for a while. Well, still, there's a lot of work to do and I suppose we're just in the way."

"Yes," says Louisa, "we probably are."

April 1912

Ruby Nill Rowbarge was as misnamed as a female scarlet tanager, in that this half of the species isn't scarlet at all but greenish, and not even greenish enough to make a noise about. Still, it's a commonplace that people's names are chosen years before there is anything much to go on. The determining factor is parental whimsy—or perhaps, to put it more kindly, artless parental confidence that the infant will grow up to embody all the name's delightful implications. No doubt Ruby was attractive enough as a baby—"enough" doesn't have to be much for babies—and so to call her Ruby must have seemed not completely irrational. But later on, to anyone who cared about such things, the name appeared more ironic than otherwise. So do we say to each other when we meet out walking in a downpour, "Fine weather we're having," and, with a caustic laugh, pass on. Ruby was not a glowing, precious stone. She was merely a stone, like thousands of others, and she, at least, never expected more. Irony was not in her, or caustic laughter, either. She accepted all things as they were.

And things, at least on the surface, were fine, for the Pleasure Dome was flourishing. Besides the new merry-go-round, which had arrived the same year as the twins, there was, by 1912, a Ferris wheel, and a terrifying thing called a Tilt-A-Wheel that tipped you nearly on your head, and another ride called a Flying Saucer that whirled you around till you were almost too dizzy to stand. There were boats, too, and frozen custard, and popcorn and balloons. Everybody loved it, and all summer long the place was full. Some people even said it was better than the Euclid Beach Park up in Cleveland, and indeed, it seemed it must be. On the Fourth of July in 1911, Herbert and Dick had grossed five thousand dollars. In just one day alone. It was amazing.

Ruby knew it was amazing, and she was grateful to Herbert, wise and clever Herbert, for marrying her. She was grateful for the twins, too. She was grateful for the fine new house he was building, for the cook, the maid, the nurse. When he left her untouched at night, as he nearly always did, she sometimes wept, very quietly so as not to disturb his sleep, but she didn't blame him for his coldness. Instead, she blamed herself for what she privately confessed was the deadly sin of lust. She was deeply ashamed of her body's wicked desires, and on Sundays, in church, she would pray for forgiveness.

She would pray, also, in church, that her husband might be happy. For she'd built around Herbert a saving little fantasy in which she saw him as the victim of a tragic love affair endured before she'd met him. That he was heartless by nature she couldn't and wouldn't allow; that he had long ago given half his heart away, this she could bear and even call romantic. Her fantasy was close to the mark, and Herbert, if he'd known of it, would have been amazed by her insight, since he sometimes, with horror and confusion, thought the very same thing himself. It was tied up, somehow, with mirrors and the sense of going mad rather than with the shadow of a long-lost woman. But however it defined itself, he had never shared it with Ruby. Too bad. She could, perhaps, have helped him. Sometimes Ruby saw with remarkable clarity. But even when that happened, her confidence was such that she could never defend her philosophies, even supposing she constructed them, and instead called vision by another, apologetic name—her woman's intuition—and kept it to herself.

So what could Ruby do? She wished above all things to do something, and knew from her constant reading that out there in the world there were women who were making big impressions. There were novelists, like Mary Roberts Rinehart; and that woman over in France, Marie Something-or-other, was even a scientist. And look at little Mary Pickford! Ruby wondered sadly how they managed it. But, of course, she said to herself, she'd never been clever. No reason to think she could be clever now.

And she wasn't athletic, either. Opal had taken up lawn tennis, and was talking of buying a bicycle. But Ruby felt clumsy rushing about on the grass, and as for cycling, one had to wear these new serge bloomers, and Ruby was sure she'd look ridiculous. She'd gotten a little fat now, since the birth of the twins. And anyway, all that exercise—well, one got so damp!

So when she wasn't mothering the twins—and the nurse was so possessive of them, so certain of knowing better than she did what was right for them, that Ruby didn't have much mothering to do—she read sentimental novels by the dozens, and began a collection of things that were pink. Anything at all would do: a mussel shell, a ribbon, a rose made of wax, or a pebble from the roadside—all were brought lovingly home and tucked into a box she kept hidden in the attic. She never told Herbert or Opal about it; she knew they would laugh at her. But the box came to seem to contain all her girlhood dreams of romance, her girlhood notions of everything pure and feminine. It was as far from reality as it could possibly be—light-years from the heavy, wet gymnastics of lovemaking, light-years from her thickening face and figure that had never worn and never would wear gauze and dance on tiptoe in the moonlight. Ruby knew it. "But," she told herself, "my soul is different," and was thrilled by the thought, thrilled that she could even have conceived of it. She decided she could have been a poet if "things" had been otherwise—what "things" she never catalogued— and it gave her life a nicely tragic resonance.

It was, of course, profoundly tragic, this life of Ruby's—and profoundly commonplace. But how could she know how commonplace it was? Just as she kept her desolation to herself, so did countless others like her, each one assuming all the others were living, as the old tales have it, happily ever after. It was her own fault, she supposed, if she was dull and plain and could not keep her husband rapturous. Yet, having failed in this, she was completely cut adrift—no other goal had ever been suggested. Life was long. She sighed, sometimes, to think how long it was. But at the end, she vowed, she'd lie and breathe her last by candlelight, with roses on her bosom, claiming in death the sweet romance that life denied her.

And then, in April of 1912, when the twins were only five years old, she died so suddenly that she was mercifully spared any knowledge of the dreary picture death made of her after all. She had just stepped round to Opal's, down the road, on an evening dim with mist, to borrow the daily paper, for Herbert, as usual, was late in coming home with a copy of his own. But there had been a terrible accident somewhere out on the ocean—a ship full of glamorous people had rammed an iceberg and gone down—and she wanted to read the story. As she was hurrying back, there was, behind her, a sudden rush of horse and wheels, and a wagon leapt out of the mist. Alarmed, she stumbled, fell forward, and a wild hoof snapped her spine in two. She was found an hour later sprawled in the road, her skirts flung up, her bloomers splashed with mud. It was, at last, an unattractive death. Not in the least romantic.

But history closed gently over Ruby. No one ever said to her daughters that she had been a fool. People hardly mentioned her at all. So Babe and Louisa grew up building fantasies around her, just as she had built her own around their father, and they always assumed that he had grieved for her.

Herbert had not grieved for her. He wanted to, but he couldn't, not even at the funeral. In fact, since the twins were too little to fully comprehend their loss, it seemed as if Dick was the only one to feel the death at all. As for Opal, she and Ruby had never much been friends—there was always something scratchy between them that kept them in a state of itch whenever they were together. And old man Nill, near death himself of cancer—a malady that shortly bore him off—was simply never told. Walter was only two; what was an aunt to him? Why, merely nothing. And Frank Festeen, who was thirteen now, well, Frank was sorry. But more for his father than for Mrs. Rowbarge. For he knew that her death recalled hard things for his father. Lollie was often brought into their conversations, and always with love and sorrow, but for Frank, that was as far as this new misfortune went. He had not known Mrs. Rowbarge very well. Not very well at all. He could not cry for her.

But Dick was stricken. "Oh, Bertie, Bertie," he said to Herbert, "it seems like you and I are just doomed, somehow. First no folks, and now no wives. Thank God we've got our children, Bertie. That's a lot. We got to be thankful for that, anyway."

"Yes, that's right," said Herbert stiffly. "That's certainly right."

They were walking away from the burial as they talked, far back from the rest of the party, and Dick's eyes were red and wet. But Herbert's, though he had the grace to be shamed by the fact, were dry.

"Bertie," said Dick, "I wish there was something I could do for you. I know it seemed sometimes like you didn't care for Ruby, but that's just your way. Why, she was a real nice person, and she loved you very much. I think that's one of the things I liked the best about her was the way she loved you."

"Yes. Well." It was all Herbert could think of to say.

They walked along in silence past the gravestones for a little distance. And then Dick said, musingly, "You'll feel better after a while, Bertie. It kind of goes away some, and you get so you feel better."

Herbert at last exploded. "For heaven's sake, Dick, keep quiet, can't you? You know perfectly well I don't feel anything. Not anything. I'm sorry for that, but it's the truth. Good grief, you know why I married Ruby, you were *there!* Don't try to make something else out of it."

Dick stopped then, and turned to face him. "Bertie," he said sadly, "you got no heart at all, do you? I've always loved you, and I always will. But I guess you can't love anybody back, can you? Not me, or Ruby, or anybody. You got no heart in there"—tapping him mournfully on the chest—"you got no heart to give."

Herbert's face went pale, for it seemed as if Dick's tapping finger had pushed a closed door open. "Listen, Dick," he said in a rush, the words tumbling out through the crack. "Sometimes I think there *is* something wrong with me. Oh, God, sometimes I think I'm going crazy. I tried to love Ruby, I really did, but I was lonely and she couldn't . . . she never understood. Dick, you got to help me, you got to stand by me. Sometimes I get this terrible, horrible feeling that I'm only . . ." He paused, not knowing how to describe it.

Dick peered at him, puzzled and concerned. "Only what, Bertie? I don't see what you mean."

But, abruptly, the moment had passed, the door swung shut again. Herbert turned away. "Never mind," he mumbled. "Never mind."

They took up their walk once more, among the weedy monuments, and at last Dick put his arm through Herbert's. "There's nothing wrong with you, Bertie," he said soberly. "I'm sorry I said that about you not having any heart. Of course you got a heart.

It's just you've had a sad life, and so have I, and this is the saddest day of all. But we got our children and we got each other. Why, shoot, in some ways we're luckier than a lot of other people."

But Herbert did not respond, so Dick dropped his arm and went along beside him thoughtfully toward home.

Dick hoped after this that he and Herbert would be brothers again, more brothers than they'd been since the old days at the Home. But he was disappointed. Herbert could not bear to recall his outburst in the graveyard. For weeks he could not face Dick without embarrassment, and turned from his outstretched hand a hundred times. Finally Dick, deciding it was best to leave him to himself for a while, drew apart, spending his free time more and more with Frank and Frank's affairs. Of course he would stand by Bertie, and help him all he could—but sometimes he wondered, reluctantly, if he'd been right in what he'd said, after all. Maybe it was true that his beloved little brother had no heart.

Tuesday, May 27, 1952

Babe and Louisa drift peacefully on the warm brown water of Red Man Lake. They have rowed—with Louisa at the oars—past the park's pavilion, where stacks of benches and tables, legs every which way, wait for arrangement; past the swimming place, where a dump truck has dropped its jaw to vomit a sliding hill of fresh, new sand—if sand is ever new —which workmen rake over the remnants of last year's imitation beach to fashion this year's imitation beach. They have rowed past cottages with patchy lawns fresh and still uncluttered, where here and there somebody mows or hammers, getting ready for the summer. And now they have come to a quiet place where two tiny islands hump together, sharing the shade of trees and a broad green dimpled skirt of lily pads.

The ping of the hammers, the voices of the sand rakers, though half a mile behind them, echo thin and sharp across the water and make their isolation sweeter. Louisa has stowed the oars, and now the sisters—bare-legged, sandal-shod, in blue culottes and matching flowered shirts—sprawl blissfully and let the boat go where it will, with the result that it has wandered into the lily pads, which stroke its sides with little whispers, parting at the bow, closing at the stern, till the boat, embraced, settles to a stop.

This is their favorite place of many on the lake, and it is nicest now, in May, before the reentry of mosquitoes, fishermen, and lovers. They came here when they were children, sometimes with a picnic to eat in the boat. They have brought a picnic today. Or, rather, Louisa has brought a picnic, having wrested from Fawn, in a burst of courage, leftover chicken from the night before, pretzels, brownies, and a thermos of lemonade.

"So Fawn said how come we don't have something better to do than lollygag around in a boat," Louisa reports.

"There *isn't* anything better to do," says Babe. "This is the best thing of all."

"That's what *I* think," says Louisa. "But I did feel kind of embarrassed. I mean, there she is, slaving away, and here we are, enjoying ourselves."

"You sound downright Communistic," says Babe severely. "It's not as if we never did *anything*. We're entitled to *some* fun, aren't we? And anyway, Fawn likes to slave."

"Do you think so?" says Louisa.

"Of course," says Babe. "Look what a big thing she

makes of it. Why, we could do what she does in half the time with half the fuss." She is not entirely certain of this, however, and so falls silent. They turn their faces up to the sun, eyes closed against the glare, and for a time neither says a word.

At last Babe says, "How's the Tunnel of Love? Is it finished?"

Louisa rights her head and, rubbing her neck, says, "Almost, I guess. When Daddy came back yesterday, he was cross because he got pink paint on his shoe from the ticket booth, and they always do the ticket booth last. At least, they always used to." She dips a hand into the water and adds, "It used to be so much fun, going down to look at new rides before they opened. Remember? Why, we haven't done that since . . ."

When she hesitates, Babe straightens up and frowns at her. "Since that time in the Fun House, you mean."

"Well, yes," says Louisa. "I'm sorry, Babe. I didn't mean to bring it up."

"Now, listen," says Babe. "That was a thousand years ago. Water over the dam. I wish you wouldn't act as if I was covered with open sores about it. Suppose I *had* married Frank after that? What would *you* have done? And anyway, it wouldn't have worked. I decided that, ages ago."

"Did you really, Babe?" asks Louisa earnestly.

"I really did," Babe assures her. "So it's all right."

"I'm glad," says Louisa simply.

They sit for a while, staring off in different directions, and then Louisa says, "Daddy didn't want you to marry Frank, anyway."

"No," says Babe. "I've never seen him so mad, before or since. He was practically purple."

"I know," says Louisa. "He scared me to death."

Babe says indignantly, "You'd have thought Frank and I were . . . well, what I mean is, all we were doing was kissing."

"I know," says Louisa.

"Oh, well," says Babe with a sigh. "Water over the dam. How is he after yesterday, speaking of scaring people?"

"He seems all right," says Louisa. "He yelled at Fawn this morning when the coffee wasn't ready, but she yelled right back. Walter was there for breakfast and they talked about christening the Tunnel of Love. Honestly—Walter! You know what he wanted Daddy to do? Break a bottle of champagne over the first boat. Like christening an ocean liner. But Daddy said he didn't want broken glass all over the place for people to step on, and a mess on the boat seats. So they're just going to cut a ribbon, and Daddy'll take the first ride, same as always. Want to go down and watch?"

"Sure," says Babe. And then she says, softening, "Poor Daddy. It's kind of touching to see him on one of his rides. He always gets that sweet, foolish look on his face, all serious and childlike both at once. I love to see him like that."

"Me, too," says Louisa. "He's always so *nice* when he's at the park."

"Well," says Babe with a shrug, "he loves it. It makes him happy."

Again they fall silent. Louisa leans out of the boat and, brow furrowed, measures the palm of her hand against the leathery, upturned palm of a lily pad. "Babe," she says at last, "when we're left alone . . ." Her voice trails off.

Babe waits, watching her, thinking: That's the way *I* look. Just like that.

"When we're left alone someday," Louisa says again, the lily pad warm under her fingers, "what will we do?"

"Well," says Babe, "I suppose we'll do what we want."

Louisa thinks this over and then says, "But what *do* we want?"

"I suppose we only want to be together," says Babe slowly. "I suppose if we were together—without Daddy, I mean—it wouldn't much matter what we did. Because once we're left alone, we won't be . . . *alone* anymore."

Louisa gives the lily pad a final stroke and sits up to face her sister. "We've always done the very best we could for Daddy," she says.

"Yes. We have," says Babe.

"We've always loved him," says Louisa.

"Always," says Babe. "But he—"

"Don't say it," says Louisa quickly. "Please don't say it, Babe. He's *needed* us, anyway. He couldn't have done without us. Don't you think so?"

"I don't know," says Babe. "I guess it doesn't mat-

ter. He's had us, whether he needed us or not."
Louisa looks away, at this, and Babe adds, "I only
meant we've been a family, you know. There when
we *do* need each other."

"I guess so," says Louisa.

"Someday, when we're . . . left alone," says Babe,
smiling now, "we'll kick up our heels. Throw wild
parties. Get Walter to bring over some of his friends,
and all get drunk."

"Babe!" Louisa gasps. "Are you serious?"

"I don't know," says Babe. "I guess not."

"Anyway," says Louisa, "it's not going to happen
tomorrow. Like you said, it could be twenty years
from now."

"So what?" says Babe. "You can get drunk any
time, even in a wheelchair."

Louisa looks shocked, but Babe is still smiling, and
finally Louisa smiles, too.

"The thing is," says Babe, "we'll be able to do anything we want. If I'd married Frank, I'd be all tied
down to the greenhouse now, and carrying bedpans
for poor old Mr. Festeen."

"And be all in a fuss about being a mother-in-law
to little Tammie Hannengraff," Louisa adds.

"That's right," says Babe. "Good grief—imagine
that! So you'd have to kick up your heels all alone."

"Now, wait a minute," says Louisa. "I might've
got married, too, you know. I might've married
Tommy Oglesby, maybe, or even Dwight. Remember
Dwight?"

"Sure," says Babe, "but you didn't. And a good

thing, too. No, it's much better this way, just the two of us. Why, someday we'll be really free!"

They tilt their faces up to the sun again, eyes shut, heads full of vague but interesting visions. After a time, Louisa stretches out her legs and one foot bumps the picnic basket. "Hey," she says, "want to eat our lunch now?"

"Pretty soon," says Babe. "We ought to work on our tans some more first."

"Well," says Louisa, "whenever you're ready." And then she adds, dreamily, "Babe, the brownies have walnuts. And frosting."

"Oh, lovely," says Babe, without opening her eyes. "That's just lovely."

Summer 1925

When, in April of 1918, Frank sailed off to France to fight the Germans, he was a red-cheeked, sturdy, gregarious child of nineteen, elated with his man's gear and his man's mission. Home again in December with a minor shoulder wound, he was still sturdy, but his cheeks were never red again in the way they'd been before, and he was no longer gregarious. He had seen things in the Argonne Forest that only his father could understand, and they sat out the long winter evenings in a silence that groaned with shared cognitions.

The months of their separation had been terrible for Dick, so much so that at forty-six he looked already old. He had been sure Frank would die "over there," and hated that foolish cock's crow of a song that he must listen to everywhere he went. But Frank had come home, he was all right, and they found themselves gentle with each other in ways that had new reverberations. Frank was, now, suddenly aware of his father's stump as the sign of something gained, not something missing, though what it was he had gained Frank couldn't have put into words. But they shared it, just the same, and understood each other.

France had, in some ways, been good for Frank, however. It had taken the red from his cheeks, but it had firmed him up, and left him rather handsome in a wholesome Ohio way. He went to work at the Pleasure Dome, to "learn the business," and was industrious and earnest in every task assigned to him, while every night he stayed at home with Dick in the cottage Dick and Herbert had lived in when they first came to Mussel Point. It was larger now, and modernized—a second story added, and a bathroom —but it was still a simple place, not like the Rowbarge house three miles away.

"Why don't you move out of that dump?" Herbert would say to Dick, with every passing year.

And Dick would always answer, "Why should I, Bertie? I like it."

And that would be that.

But there was money in the bank, more money than Dick had ever dreamed of, and when Frank came home from France, Dick, to celebrate, and without saying anything to anyone, went out and bought sixty acres of farmland outside Mussel Point, and thought, at night, of cows.

"Dad," said Frank one night at supper in the early spring, "you know, the park is nice and all that, but, gee, I don't know. Sometimes it seems kind of . . . well, I don't want to hurt your feelings if you like it as much as Mr. Rowbarge does, but . . . well, sometimes it seems kind of *foolish* to me."

Next morning Dick went out and bought a tractor.

During the seven years that followed, the Rowbarge twins grew up. And one Sunday night in '25, at dinner with the Looses, Opal said, "Herbert, what are you going to do about these girls?"

"Do about them?" said Herbert, glancing at Babe and Louisa where they sat side by side across the table. He glanced at them as seldom as possible, and never without the same dull resentment that had settled in his stomach on the day they were born. Still: "What's the matter with them?" he demanded. "They look all right." They looked, in fact, not at all like Ruby, and he wondered, sometimes, who they *did* look like. They were of medium height, like Ruby, but unlike him or Ruby, they were big-boned, and wide of hip and mouth. And their hair was a funny shade of tan. He had once told Opal they resembled his Cincinnati aunt, but to himself he observed uneasily that there was something inelegant about their looks, something that was not, on the whole, hightoned. They were good girls, though, and never gave him trouble. It might, he admitted to himself, have been far worse.

Opal had had her hair bobbed the week before, and the change was not successful. She was aware of this and it made her even sharper than usual. "Good grief, Herbert, open your eyes," she said now, impatiently. "They're eighteen years old, and it's time you gave a minute of your precious time to planning for their future. Do you intend to send them to college?"

"College!" said Herbert. "What for?"

"Why, to educate them. You've heard of education?"

"They're educated," he said. "My God, they just graduated from high school."

"And I suppose you think that's enough."

"Well, Opal, it was enough for you and their mother," he said mildly.

"Honestly, Herbert," she sighed. "That was the Dark Ages. Nobody went, back then. But lots of girls go to college now. I'd go in a minute if I was their age."

Stuart helped himself to more mashed potatoes, and boomed, "Watch out, Herbert, old man! Since the ladies got the vote, they're getting mighty bold!"

"Oh, be quiet, Stuart, and eat your dinner," Opal snapped, and Walter, who was fifteen now, guffawed. But no one told Walter to be quiet. No one ever had.

Babe and Louisa sat looking back and forth as the talk went on. College? It might be fun. But if Daddy was against it . . . Babe was a little firmer than Louisa, but neither was so firm as to oppose him.

"Well, I think it's a lot of foolishness," said Herbert, "and I'm not going to do it. They're fine just the way they are."

"All right," said Opal. "Very good. But then you'd better get going and find husbands for them somewhere."

"Oh, for heaven's sake, Opal," said Herbert. "They can find their own husbands."

"Around here? There aren't any nice young men around here. Not a single solitary one. Unless you want them to marry hayseeds."

"Let 'em marry Frank Festeen," said Walter gleefully. "They're both sweet on him."

"We are not!" said Babe.

And Herbert said, "Frank? Oh, come now, Walter. Where'd you get a notion like that? That's nonsense."

But, after dinner, Opal took Herbert aside. "Walter doesn't miss much, in case you didn't know it," she told him. "If he says the girls are sweet on Frank, I expect he's probably right."

"Well?" said Herbert impatiently. "What if they are? My God, Opal, they're only children, after all."

"Herbert, I swear sometimes I think you've got just enough sense to run the park and none left over for anything else. They're *eighteen*. When I was eighteen, I was *engaged*. Now, look, Frank's a nice boy and all that, but he's got no background any more than Dick does. The Nill name has always stood for something in this county, and it's up to all of us to take pride in it and protect it."

Though most of the time he didn't like Opal, Herbert had always respected her. He had watched her, and learned a great deal from her, and now he chewed a thumb thoughtfully. On the whole, he had to admit he agreed with her assessment of Dick and Frank. Rich as Dick was, he'd never made the slightest effort to improve himself. He hadn't sent Frank to college, or built a decent house, or anything.

Opal, observing him closely, saw and pressed her advantage. "And of course you'll want to protect the Rowbarge name, Herbert," she said. "I'm sure you don't want farmers in the family, either. Oh, I know, Dick's your partner, but he started out pretty low, or so you've told me, and it's just not suitable to think of taking his son into the family."

"I suppose you're right, Opal," said Herbert. "No, it wouldn't be a good thing. I've known Dick all my life, but still . . ."

"What goes on between you men," said Opal, "with all your back-slapping and cigars and filthy stories, is entirely your own affair. But when it comes to family, that's something else again."

"All right, Opal," he said. "I'll keep my eyes open. You're right—when the girls do get married, it's got to be to people at our own level." He said it, and believed it was proper. He and Dick, well, they were different from each other. They'd always been different, right from the beginning. Both orphans, yes, but that was where it ended. And now, recalling this, his resentment of his daughters pricked him anew. Drag down everything by marrying Frank Festeen? Certainly not. "But," he added aloud to Opal, "I still can't believe there's anything serious in it. Those girls—they hardly know how to pull up their socks. In love! Why, it's got to be nonsense!"

But it was not nonsense. For Babe *was* in love with Frank, and Louisa, who loved him too, though not, they agreed, so much, was generously set on helping. At night, in the room they insisted on sharing, they crimped their hair, tried rolling their stockings, and talked of nothing else. Frank was handsome and dear and good, they told each other. So what if he hadn't gone to college like Daddy and Uncle Stuart? That didn't make him a hayseed. Why, Frank was raising flowers on that farm out there, not just oats and corn. And there was talk of a greenhouse someday. No, he was certainly not a hayseed. Babe loved him, and they would find a way to make him love her back. And marry her. Soon. But—what if Daddy didn't like it? Well, my goodness, wasn't Frank the son of Daddy's dearest friend? And business partner? Of course Daddy would like it. So, when an opportunity came, one day in the Fun House, they reached out eagerly and took it.

The town of Mussel Point and Red Man Lake were not, that summer, what they once had been. Before the Pleasure Dome, when Herbert had first scouted out the site in 1900, he had walked along the dusty country roads, past endless shabby farms, and if he hadn't had his map in hand, he'd never have known there was anything so wet and lovely as a lake ahead. The only clues were clumsy little signs, two or three, on farmhouse gates, advertising the sale of worms for fishing. And then the road made a sudden turn and there it lay, enormous, brown, serene, with tiny islands—a quiet place and almost all untouched. And the town was a thin collection of cottages and stores, presided over by the Nill National Bank. A center for the farmers in the countryside around, nothing more.

But now the town was fat, and the lake was no longer serene. In fact, if you were coming down from Lima or Ada, or over from Wapakoneta, you couldn't even see the water, for the Pleasure Dome was built along that side and hid the shore from view. What you did see, first off, was the parking lot.

The parking lot—vast, unpaved, and lumpy—was by itself a marvel. All day long and far into the night the cars roared in and out, spraying pebbles and keeping the thick summer dust so agitated that it hardly ever got a chance to settle, but swirled in coarse tan clouds from Memorial Day on the one end till Labor Day on the other. And if this was a marvel, the park itself was a miracle, for Herbert had made of it a huge and living thing, a snarling, glorious, dreadful, magical thing stretched out a half a mile along the water's edge and bounded by a place where he had spread rough yellow sand and made a beach for swimming. It was an act of creation, but he never would have wished it done in seven days. Why should he want it to be finished? The world, he sometimes thought, could have used another day or two of work; he would not stint, himself. He tinkered with his Garden ceaselessly, uprooting this and adding that, refurbishing and staking, testing its fruits—in this case, frozen custard and popcorn—and tending with paternal pride his flock of employees. He was everywhere at once, and nowhere so often as at the merry-go-round.

The merry-go-round was the same one he'd had since 1907. There were bigger ones available, of course—much bigger. But he did not like the bigger ones. Their animals stepped round in ranks of three or four. Pairs were what he'd wanted, were what he still wanted. It was, as it had always been, his Noah's Ark, his Peaceable Kingdom, and, with its shrill calliope, the speaking heart of his soul's own country.

There were many other rides, of course. In addition to the Tilt-A-Wheel, the Ferris wheel, and the Flying Saucer, still big attractions, there was a lethal machine called the Whip that flung you around a figure-eight-shaped track and nearly snapped your head off. There was the Aeroplane, which opened like an umbrella and whirled you out sidewise. There was a ride called the Bullet that closed you into a sort of cage and swung you up and around on a long steel arm while the cage itself revolved, so that some of the time you were upside down. And of course, soaring on skinny stilts, there was the scalloping, endless spine of a roller coaster, like a Loch Ness monster's skeleton bleached white and perilously flimsy in the glaring summer sun. Along this narrow track, all day and far into the night, a little train of linked red cars clanked up and hurtled down the scallops, and just above the gates to the park, the track rose to its highest point, a dizzy, crazy height, and doubled back on itself down a grade so steep it was a wonder anyone survived it.

The shooting gallery was still there, though twice rebuilt and expanded, and many other games involving missiles to hurl at targets. There was a Penny Arcade, with an eerie mechanical gypsy who could tell your fortune. There were even, for the littlest customers, ponies, plumed and docile, to ride around a ring. And now, this year, there was a brand-new thing—a Fun House.

If the merry-go-round was the heart of the park, the Fun House was its brain, an unhinged brain that suited the park exactly. For it was not so much a Fun House as a madhouse, a place of chaos and hysteria, with steps that switched to ramps and back again, and rocking floors, and little rooms constructed fiendishly to warp your sense of gravity and distance and send you bouncing off their walls. It had a twisting, mirrored maze so disorienting that you walked right into yourself before you knew it, and bumped your nose. There were little holes in the

floors from which sharp jets of air would suddenly
blow your clothes up, and sirens, just as sudden,
that deafened you. It was, said Herbert happily, a
dilly. It was also, on the day before it opened, the
residence of Fate.

They all came down that day to try it out—Dick and
Herbert, Babe and Louisa, and the Looses. And Frank
came over from the farm. It had become a ritual, this
viewing of new attractions. While the park roared
on around them, and visitors paused to wonder who
these privileged people were, they would slip behind
the canvas shroud obscuring whatever the new thing
was and give it a cheerful inspection. And it was
always aptly timed: too late to make the alterations
Opal would invariably suggest. "It should have been
red, not blue," she would say, or "It should have
been faster." Or slower. "Well, maybe next time,
Opal," Herbert would answer. "Too late to change
it now." And she would say, "You should have let me
see it sooner," and he would nod and say he wished
he had. And then it would open and be a huge
success.

This time it was a little different, for the Fun
House was not a game or a ride but a cluster of
lunatic jolts. Dick, with his crutch, stayed just inside
the entrance. Not for him steps that turned into
ramps, and rocking floors. Opal and Stuart circled
its small central room, exclaiming at their reflections
in crazy mirrors that stretched their necks or gave
them legs like barrels. Walter went off to test the

buttons that controlled the sirens and the jets of air. Herbert stayed with Dick, discussing possible improvements. And Louisa and Babe and Frank went through an archway to the mirrored maze, and disappeared.

Ten minutes passed, then twenty. At last Louisa emerged, alone. "Where's Babe?" said Herbert. "Or Louisa. Or whichever."

"I'm Louisa, Daddy," she said brightly. "Babe'll be out in a minute."

"Go get her," he said. "It's time we were going along."

"She'll be out in just a minute," said Louisa. Her brightness faded and she began to twist her fingers nervously.

"Is she lost in there?"

"Oh, no, Daddy. You can't really get lost," she said quickly. "I'm sure she'll be right out."

"Frank's in there, too," said Dick. "He'll take care of her."

At this, Opal looked at Herbert, raised her eyebrows pointedly, and said, "Ahem."

"Oh," he said. He went down the steps that turned into a ramp—hopped down, with care—and crossed the little room. "I'll get her," he said. "I ought to check things out in there, anyway. I haven't seen it since they finished up."

"No, Daddy, wait!" wailed Louisa. "I'll go—you don't have to bother."

"Stay where you are," said Herbert, and he went through the archway into the maze.

It was a terrible mistake. The instant he went in among the mirrors, he knew it and cursed himself for a fool. Everywhere he looked, in this labyrinth of narrow passages, he saw himself: walking toward himself, beside himself, coming and going at angles. The dreaded, half-sought-for twinkling down his spine began, intensified, was suddenly unbearable. Alarmed, he tried to hurry, groping his way along with sweating hands, and saw his own blanched face and staring eyes reflected at every turn. He felt all at once a queer desire to sink to the floor, to give in, to stay there babbling at himself forever—a desire so overwhelming that his panic doubled. "Damn them," he gasped unreasonably, "it's all their fault." And then, from over his head, a siren shrieked, and his thudding heart lurched crazily. "My God," he whispered. "Oh, my God." He began to run, caroming off the mirrored walls while a dozen Herberts did the same. He rushed into his own embrace with arms outstretched, fell backward, and sat down heavily to gape with a joy more horrible than horror at the gaping Herberts all around him. With a final burst of will, he picked himself up, and, rounding a sort of corner, reeled into a cubicle. And there he saw before him an endless, measureless corridor tapering far off into infinity. Leaning along it was an endless row of Babes and an endless row of Frank Festeens. And she was kissing him.

At once his fear turned bottom up, exploding into rage. With a strangled exclamation, he grabbed for her arm and spun her around, and somehow found the route back to the archway, dragging her, terrified, behind him. "Your boy's in there," he said to Dick in a voice that froze even Opal in her tracks. "Send him home. I'll speak to you later on this. Tonight."

"Do you love her?" asked Dick.

And Frank said, "Well, I've always liked her, Dad. Liked 'em both. They're nice kids. But I don't think I exactly *love* Babe, to be honest with you. No."

"Then why were you kissing her?"

"Well, I wasn't, that's just it," Frank explained. "I mean, we were acting kind of silly, sure. She was dancing around, making faces in the mirrors and things like that, and then all at once she sort of tripped, and I caught her, and, well, all of a sudden she kissed *me!*"

"He may say you have to marry her," said Dick sadly. "He looked pretty upset."

"Then of course I'll do it," Frank said. "If it's what she wants."

"You'll stay away from him, do you hear me?" said Herbert in a voice that was still unsteady. "You'll stay completely away."

"It wasn't his fault," Babe sobbed. "It was me. I did it."

"I know that," said Herbert coldly. "That was perfectly plain, and I'm ashamed of you. I hope you're ashamed of yourself. What are you, anyway? Some kind of easy woman?" Like your mother, he almost added. Or mine, he almost let himself think. And he sent her upstairs, where for hours she wept in her sister's arms.

Herbert knew he had behaved unreasonably, had blown the thing up out of all proportion. He had blown it up, in fact, to fit the proportion of his panic in the maze, and thinking of that, unwillingly, on his way to talk to Dick, he shuddered and wondered how long it would be before the madness he had so long expected would finally overtake him.

To Dick he said, tiredly, "It won't do, of course."

"No," said Dick, profoundly relieved.

"She's too young."

"Yes, there's that, and also, Bertie, they're not in love. Not really."

"*He* isn't, anyway," said Herbert.

"No, he's not. I'm sorry, Bertie."

"It will all blow over," said Herbert. He stood up and said, more firmly, "I'm going to have that maze torn out, though, Dick. We don't want it turning into a spot where these young people think they can go to spoon."

"You're probably right," said Dick. "You could put something else back there."

"Yes, add some more contraptions. Of course, that means putting off the opening."

"Well," said Dick, "that's all right. Another month or two won't matter." There was a pause, and then Dick said, "Bertie, I been wanting to talk to you anyway, so I'm glad you came over. I want to pull out. Out of the park, I mean."

"Why? What's the matter?"

"Nothing, only I'm fifty-three, Bertie. And I'm tired. I want to go out to the farm, with Frank. I can't do much real farming, just like you said before we came here, when we sold out down to Gaitsburg. But Frank wants to start the greenhouse, Bertie. And—I want to do it with him."

"Back to the farm," said Herbert. "Dick, you haven't changed at all."

"No, I guess I haven't."

"Well, the park's half yours. I'll buy you out."

"No—no, don't do that. I already got more money than is good for me."

"Dick, don't be an ass. I'll get a lawyer on it and see what's fair, and I'll buy you out. If you really mean what you say."

"Yes, Bertie, my mind's made up."

"Well, we came a long way together."

"Yep."

"Just a couple of damned orphans."

"Yep."

Herbert said, then, "I'm grateful to you, Dick, for keeping all my secrets."

"Well, Bertie, there never was anything I wouldn't do for you. You know that."

"Yes, I guess I do." For an instant Herbert was on the brink of telling Dick about the Fun House, about what had really happened to him in the mirrored maze and the real reason why he wanted to tear it out. But just in time he backed away from it. What was the use? They clapped each other on the back, shook hands, and said good night.

Frank married Myra Dillon, a girl from the next farm up, the following summer. It was, said Opal to Herbert, a very appropriate match. It was, said Babe to Louisa, the end of everything.

Wednesday afternoon, May 28, 1952

Babe Rowbarge stands at the counter in Aunt Opal's kitchen, cutting olives on a board. Arranged on a platter at her elbow are little rounds of toast, heaped with mayonnaise and tuna, and she tops each one with half an olive set cut side up so that its bright red nubbin of pimento can be seen to full advantage. Beside her waits a tea cart made of gold-toned metal, with two glass shelves. The top shelf holds Aunt Opal's silver tea service, glowing from its morning rubdown and flanked by tiny linen napkins, a plate of lemon slices, and four cups and saucers of fluted porcelain thin as the shells of eggs. The cups and saucers have been handed down from a grandmother brought as a bride to Ohio, protesting all the way, from far-off, more civilized Connecticut. The silver is Aunt Opal's own, bought whole and entire in Cleveland.

Babe sinks the last half olive into place and, stooping, sets the platter on the bottom shelf of the tea cart beside matching platters of coconut macaroons and fruit-betty bars dusted with powdered sugar. These last are something new she has made from an enthusiastic recipe in a magazine. They look all right, but on the whole she thinks she won't repeat the effort. It took an hour to dice the figs, prunes, dates, and nuts, a fact the recipe has chosen to suppress.

"There!" says Babe, standing up to admire the full effect. Then she goes to the swinging door and pushes it open to listen. It is Aunt Opal's turn to host Wednesday bridge, and from the card room the steady talk of the women, interspersed with moans and cries and brief, intense silences as crucial cards are played, has not yet come to a climax. "Shoot," says Babe to herself. "Too soon to boil the water." She lets the door swing to, and leans against the stove with a sigh. Oh, well, she thinks, on Sunday she'll be moving back home, and Louisa will take over here. Not that it's so much easier helping Daddy, but at least he doesn't entertain at bridge, and even if he did, Fawn would chop the fruit and shine the silver. Aunt Opal always had a girl until five years ago, but with the start of this nice arrangement with her nieces, she let the girl go except for once-a-week cleaning. "She'd just be underfoot," Aunt Opal said. "We don't really need her now."

A movement outside the window attracts Babe's attention and she peers out to see her sister waving at her. In a moment the back door opens and Louisa comes in. "I had to park on the *street*," she exclaims. "Is Wednesday bridge here today? Oh-oh"—seeing the tea cart—"I guess *so*. What'd you make? What are *those*?"

"Fruit-betty bars," says Babe.

"They look yummy," says Louisa. "What's in them?"

Babe holds out the pan in which the bars were baked, where a few broken chunks remain. "They've got everything in them," she says. "Too much trouble."

Louisa takes a chunk, tries it, and says, "They're yummy, though. Mmm—dates! Listen, Babe, I'm on my way down to Ellison's for aspirin—"

"Aspirin!" Babe interrupts. "You just bought a whole bottle!"

"Well, I know," says Louisa, "but Daddy dropped it this morning, right in the toilet, and he'd taken the cap off already, so of course they were all ruined. He broke a glass, too, last week. He's been dropping things a lot lately."

"I don't like the sound of it," says Babe. "Did you call Dr. Herdman?"

"Well, I was going to," says Louisa, "and then he seemed all right and so I didn't. What *I* think is, he's all worn out. This is the hardest time of the year, right before the park opens. He's either down there with Walter, or Walter's out at the house with *him*, and it's business, business, business all day long."

"I suppose so," says Babe. "I wish he'd slow down."

"Well, anyway, Babe," her sister continues, "I stopped by to ask you about an idea I had. For his birthday. *You* know, something to give him besides the bathrobe. They sent me over to Walter's this morning for some papers he forgot on his desk, and while I was in there I noticed that plate from Kenyon Walter's got on the radiator. With the administration building on it? And I suddenly thought what a nice thing that would be for Daddy. He's always been so proud of going to Kenyon."

"Gee, I don't know," says Babe. "He's been mad at them for a long time."

"I know," says Louisa, "but still."

"Well, maybe," says Babe. "How would you get one, though?"

"Well, I thought I could just write over there and ask," says Louisa. "There's probably a college store or something that sells them. Walter would know an address."

"Well . . . all right," says Babe. "Why not? It's a nice idea. We're going to need *something*, not to look so silly next to Walter's fancy photograph."

"That's just it," agrees Louisa. "That's just what I thought."

A voice from the living room calls, "Babe? Dear—where's our *tea*?"

"Oh, Lord," says Babe. "They're ready, and the water isn't hot." She turns the flame up high under the kettle and calls back, "Any minute, Aunt Opal."

"I better get out of your hair," says Louisa. She picks up a second chunk from the fruit-betty pan. "These are really good!" she says.

"Want to stay for tea?" asks Babe. "I'm sure it would be all right."

"Oh—no," says Louisa. "I have to get down to Ellison's." She goes to the door and then turns back. "Babe," she says, "let's see if we can get Daddy to go away for a while after the park opens. You know. Take a little vacation. He hasn't done that in years."

"When did he *ever* do it?" says Babe. "I don't remember his ever going away."

"Oh, yes, there was that one time, a while ago. A long while ago, now I come to think of it. But, Babe, the point is, he really needs a rest."

"It wouldn't be much fun for him alone," says Babe.

"Well," says Louisa, "maybe one of us could go along."

"Louisa," says her sister, "he wouldn't want that."

Louisa hesitates, and then she says, "Well, no, I guess he wouldn't."

The water in the kettle begins a rustling sound, and the voice from the other room calls again: "Babe—dear—how are things coming?"

"Two minutes, Aunt Opal," Babe calls back. "Everything's almost set."

"Well, anyway," says Louisa, "I think I'll suggest it to him. It won't do any harm."

"No, it couldn't hurt," Babe agrees.

Then, soon, Louisa gone, the tea cart wheeled in, the guests and Aunt Opal pacified, Babe returns to the kitchen, where she leans once more against the stove and, turning the pages of the magazine which contains the fruit-betty recipe, comes to an article entitled *CAN ABSENCE MAKE THE HEART GROW FONDER? Advice from Three Wives on How to Keep Romance Alive When Hubby's Job Keeps Him on the Road.* Picking at crumbs from the fruit-betty pan, Babe starts to read and is soon absorbed, as if the problems of the three in the article are pressingly her own, the wise solutions something to try herself as soon as time permits.

November 1936

In the fall of '27, Walter Loose went merrily off to Gambier, eighty miles away, to begin his freshman year at Kenyon. He came home for the holidays more full of himself than ever. College, he said, was the berries. He carried a pocket flask, demanded a roadster for Christmas, was given it, and promptly drove it into a tree. He invaded Herbert's office at the park one afternoon, "drunk as a skunk" by his own admission, and insisted that Herbert sing with him. "C'mon, Uncle Herbert, you know how it goes. 'The *first* of Kenyon's goodly *race*'—c'mon, Uncle Herbert —'was *that* great man Philander Chase.' Wassa matter? You forget the words? 'He climbed a *hill* and *said* a *pray*-ay-yer . . .' Well, never min', ol' man.

Say, listen, I tried to look you up in the annuals and I couldn' fin' you anywhere!"

Herbert, disgusted, threw Walter out of his office, but for months thereafter he was fearful that his tidy web of lies would come unraveled. He needn't have worried. Walter, it was discovered in the spring, had been drunk most of the year and had spent so little time in class that he had flunked every one of his final exams. A letter from the Dean to Stuart explained that "Walter does not have, at this time, what we look for in a student at Kenyon," and closed with the hope that Walter would be "happier at another institution." It was kindly put, but the meaning was plain. Walter had been expelled.

Stuart was heartbroken. Now there would be no medical school, no son to take over his practice. But Herbert was so relieved to know his secret would be safe that he took Walter's side at once. It was the college's fault, he argued convincingly. Why, they had exposed the boy to all these modern temptations and done nothing to protect him, and now they were punishing him for a situation that was their fault entirely. By God, he asserted, they'd never get another penny from him! He would sever all connections, remove his name from the rolls. He'd been thinking of a major gift to the Alumni Fund, but now—well, let them cry for it. And he played this scene so well, so feelingly, that Opal, grateful, looked on him with more favor than she ever had before.

Walter, at first, was as saddened as his father.

Life at Kenyon had appealed to him strongly, and now to have it denied him was a shock. Very little had ever been denied him: he was staggered by the loss, and also sobered. Still, to have his Uncle Herbert for a champion eased his soul, and when his father said he'd have to get a job to prove he could be a man, he went to Herbert's office once again and asked to be taken on.

It was the very thing, Herbert decided. Frank Festeen was settled at the greenhouse, and Babe and Louisa—what use were they? The park must be left to someone when the time came, or sold out of the family. And Herbert had always liked Walter. You couldn't help but like him, he was such a rascal. But could Walter be trained? Could he be serious, and care? He could. He took to it right away. For it was fun to be serious about the Pleasure Dome, and Walter insisted on fun.

"You know, Uncle Herbert," he said at the end of a year, "it's a lot like dreams at the Dome, I think. It's all kind of crazy and beautiful, and you can fly, and fall a long way without ever hitting the ground, and it's got those crazy mirrors where everything's all twisted out of shape. And it's mostly a night thing, like dreams, don't you think so? I mean, it's fine in the daytime, but at night, with all the colored lights and noise and people yelling, it's just . . . well, it's just amazing! Then, of course, it's like a circus, too. Like being a person in a circus where you ride the animals, like on the merry-go-round, and perform all those death-defying acts. It's just one great big party! Why, you can go in there and pay your money and do all kinds of things you'd never get away with outside. Y'know what I mean?"

Herbert knew what he meant. "I take it you like it, then?" he asked.

"You bet, Uncle Herbert. It's the nuts!"

"Well, then, Walter," said Herbert, much gratified by the boy's enthusiastic talk, "I'll make you a proposition. We'll give it another year or two, and if you're still feeling this way about it, well, you're my nephew and the logical person to take over someday. *If* you show me you can handle it."

Walter grinned. "Don't worry about that!" he declared. "I can handle it. You'll see."

"You know," said Herbert, "I do believe you can."

All through the deepest days of the Depression the Pleasure Dome thrived, for people needed fun as much as ever, more than ever. And in spite of "that man in the White House," who seemed determined to ruin everybody who wasn't ruined already, Herbert continued to prosper. But by 1936, with Walter more and more of a help, more and more eager to "handle the details" in ways that Dick had never been, Herbert had a little time on his hands—time to think. He had always kept himself too busy to think, but now he thought about his life and began to grow restless. He was fifty-six. "My God," he said to himself, "I'm getting old. In four years I'll be sixty." Sixty.

There was something about it that filled him with melancholy, something not concerned with the piling up of years so much, but rather with a sense of some vital element too long missing.

"It's just you're missing Ruby, Bertie," said Dick one night as they sat together in Frank's new house at the farm. Dick's grandson, Joe, was snugly tucked in bed upstairs, and Dick was sitting while Frank and Myra went to the movies over in Bell Fountain. *San Francisco* was playing, and "Myra can't miss a Clark Gable picture," Dick had said on the telephone. "Come on out and spend the evening with me and Joe." And Herbert had gone, gladly. Maybe Dick could ease him of his loneliness. But now, at this mention of Ruby, Herbert shook his head impatiently.

"It isn't that, Dick. Not at all."

"Well, I only meant a sense of family, you know," said Dick. "A sense of things *continuing*. Pretty soon the girls will get married and have their own kids, and then you'll feel better."

"They'll never get married," said Herbert. "They've got all they need in each other." He paused and then ventured: "No, it isn't the idea of things continuing. It's more as if things never even started. Or at least got started wrong somehow."

"Why, Bertie," said Dick, "it seems like you ought to be real satisfied. Just look what all you've done."

"Dick, I don't mean that. Not the park. Oh, I don't know." And he pulled at his chin forlornly.

"Bertie, listen. What you need is to get away," said Dick. "Go off somewhere and take a vacation.

Why, you've never really had one, all these years, with the park so much work in the summers."

"Maybe," said Herbert. "Maybe. I just don't know."

But Dick's suggestion that he get away stayed with him, and one morning in the autumn he woke up thinking that he *would* take a trip, after all. He would go back to Gaitsburg, to the Home. Maybe that was what it was, that old and growing sense of something missing. Maybe he needed to know whose son he was.

He drove across the state, one glittering Friday in November, in a brand-new Lincoln touring car. He had bought the car, he confessed to himself, to show off, to go back in style. But even so, he was nervous about going back and almost at once began to wonder if he shouldn't turn around, forget the whole idea. He took his time, while he wondered, following the rivers whenever he could—the Big Darby toward Columbus, the Scioto south to Chillicothe—rolling along with them gently down, down, down toward the wide Ohio. He stopped for coffee, for lunch, for coffee again, eating and drinking slowly, always thinking he could turn back any time he liked, and then, finding he had come all the way to Rodney, five miles from Gaitsburg, he stopped again, for gasoline this time, and lingered in the greasy office of the filling station, staring at a rack of folded maps, the flyspecked displays of fan belts and windshield-wiper blades, till at last the attendant, coming in, asked if he would move the Lincoln away from the pumps to make room for other customers. "Friday, y'know," said the boy respectfully in his soft, south-Ohio twang. "Lotsa folks be needin' gas for the weekend."

"Oh—yes," said Herbert, embarrassed. "Sorry."

"That's okay," said the boy. "She's a real nice buggy. Gave the place a little style just havin' her sit there. Where you headed?"

"Gaitsburg," said Herbert.

"Yeah? Well, you ain't got far to go, then."

Herbert climbed into the Lincoln and left the station, sitting tall in case the boy was watching, but just outside the town he slowed and pulled off the road onto the weedy berm. To his right a cow, alone in a small pasture, stood at the fence and gazed at him without surprise. The cow made him think of Dick, of all the years they had been together, slipping back from the park far into the past, back from the sharp realities of Mussel Point into the blur that Gaitsburg had long since become.

Sometimes, in bed at night, a dark, dimensionless screen far back in the endless cavern of his brain glowed briefly with flickering images, shreds of action captured on blurry film. Himself running shoeless over grass. A sunlit window. A rush of clustered faces, huge, with moving mouths. The bottom of a staircase flying up at him. But soundless. That was what his childhood had become: the remnants of a soundless movie, dim and disconnected, where, if only he could see, some answer was concealed. The Home, and Gaitsburg, had, he supposed—no, he *knew*—had substance once, but now . . . he wondered: could they really *be* there, walls and grass and windows? Had they been there all along? Or had they slid away from under him, turning with the earth, dissolving into darkness as they dropped beyond his sight? And could they now reconstitute themselves, collect from a swirl of motes and once again be real?

The question made him think of rocks. He had read somewhere that rocks at the bottom of the Grand Canyon were two thousand million years old. No signs of former life in rocks like that; just the fossils of some poor sort of algae that had grown there long before fish, long before trees, long before himself. Rows of fossil dots were all there was; delicate, like hen tracks. Barely visible. In the office at the Home, at the bottom of a stack of files piled up like the Grand Canyon's walls from a time before his consciousness, would he find a row of dots left by some fossil Rowbarge, to prove beyond doubt an evolution? And what would it mean if there was nothing?

These thoughts—he did not like these thoughts. It was as if he heard the breath of madness, that madness he feared so much, snuffling in his ears. There was something the matter. Oh, yes—he was very sure of that. But he would shrug it off. He always had before. He turned his head to find the cow still gazing at him, and for the first time in his life he envied a fellow creature's lack of comprehension.

He started up the car and drove the last four eerie

miles to find that Gaitsburg was still there. He was stunned to see how little it had changed—stunned to find that, driving through, he was not huge, a giant staring down on little images. It rose up firm and hard around him and he shrank to fit, his head, in the process, clearing and adapting. Why, what an ass he was! It was only a dingy little town, powerless to touch him. There was the depot, as disheartening as ever, and . . . well, no—the stables were gone. So was the field where he had first seen a merry-go-round. And across the square, with the same frilly little bandstand looking foolish as ever among the leafless trees, there was a wide concrete place to park now, along the riverfront, that hadn't been there before. He swung the Lincoln into it, climbed out, and stood staring across the Ohio at the West Virginia side. It seemed remote, somehow, another country—nothing but silent hills and trees—and it depressed him. He did not want to be depressed. He got back into the Lincoln and drove again around the square to the only Gaitsburg hotel.

Inside, at the desk, he signed the register for a clerk too bored to look up, and an aged bellhop carried his suitcase up a creaking flight of stairs. The room was neat and simple, but it, too, depressed him.

"Want the winda open?" asked the bellhop.

"No," said Herbert. "Not now."

"Yer the boss," said the bellhop.

Herbert gave the man a quarter, closed the door

on him, and sat down in a chair by the window, looking out. Yes, the town had changed some after all. But the changes were superficial, like new buttons on an old shirt; the fabric still scratched. From the window Herbert looked at Gaitsburg—and thought how much he'd always hated it. He stood up again and went to find a restaurant for supper.

The Riverboat Inn was almost deserted, its menu dog-eared, but he felt too tired to look for a better place. He sat down heavily at the nearest table and stared at the salt and pepper shakers, trying to remember why in the world he had come back. And then a waitress appeared.

"Hi there," she said.

Herbert looked up at her—pale cheeks rouged with bright disks of color, eyes expressionless despite the animation of her greeting—and he sighed. And then he looked again, more closely. The skin of her face was slack, and drooped a little from the bones, but there was something there—something about the tilt of the nose, the way it seemed to pull on the upper lip to reveal the wide-spaced teeth behind it— something about the elbows sharp below the stiff-starched little sleeves of her uniform. One of those elbows had bruised his ribs repeatedly, long ago. He was sure of it. There was a badge on her pocket, and he peered at it. Yes. "Esther," he said.

"That's right, honey," she said. "So! What'll it be?"

"Esther Conkling," he said.

"Say," she said, suddenly wary. "How'd *you* know?"

"I guess you don't remember me," he said, feeling foolish. "I'm Bertie Rowbarge, Esther. From the Home."

Her mouth fell open. "Jeez Louise!" she goggled. "Bertie! Sure, it's you, all right. What're *you* doin' back?"

"Oh," he said, vaguely ashamed of himself, "I just . . . I'm just passing through."

She leaned on the table and studied him. "You look pretty slick, Bertie. Say!"—she slapped his hand playfully—"remember how I use t'go after you? You was my big heartthrob, remember? Jeez, I thought you was ab-so-lute-ly *it.*"

"Well, it was a long time ago," he said. "How've you been, Esther? Didn't you ever leave here?"

Her mouth drew down at the corners, pulling the tilted nose with it. "Can you beat it?" she said. "I been here the whole damn time. Carl—that's my husband—him and me *own* this joint. We was doin' okay till '32, but now, well, business is just god-awful. We can't afford no waitresses or nothin'. He's out there now"—pointing to the kitchen—"doin' the cookin', and here I am out here. Jeez, that's the way we *started.* Well, nothin' special, at that, I guess. Hard times all over. How about you, Bertie? What *you* been doin' all this while?"

"Oh, well," he said, suddenly reluctant to tell her about it, "I'm in business up north."

"Yeah. *Good* business. I can see that." Her eyes softened. "That's nice, Bertie. I'm glad you're doin' good. You married?"

"I was," he said. "She died."

"Any kids?"

"Yes, two. Twins."

"Ya don't say! That's swell. Carl and me never did have no kids. But, Bertie, gee—I'm sorry about your wife."

"That's all right," he said, embarrassed. "It was years ago."

"Well, look," said Esther, "I better take your order, so's Carl don't think I'm goofin' off too much. But I'll come back and talk to you some more in a while. We ain't too busy these days. I guess you can see *that*."

He made a safe selection from the menu, and Esther went off through a swinging door while he sat back, pondering, to wait. Esther Conkling! She had chased him round and round the barn once, and caught him at last, and kissed him. On the mouth. No one had kissed him on the mouth for years now. He wondered if she remembered. Yes, probably she did. My, my. Esther. He pressed at the base of his skull, where a headache was slowly unfolding.

Later, with dessert, she came and sat at the table and they talked about the Home. It was nice, for once, not to pretend to be something else. Esther, watching as he tried to eat his pie, said at last, "I kissed you once, Bertie. Remember?"

"Yes," he said. "I remember."

"I sure was gone on you," she sighed. She paused, and then said, carefully, "Say, Bertie, you got a place to stay tonight? I mean, we got an extra room over at our place, and after we close up, at eight, Carl's

goin' bowling. He won't be back till midnight. And—
well—the thing is, Bertie, I still think about you a
lot—I don't know why—you'd think I'da got over
you by now—but I always thought if I ever got half
a chance . . ." She paused and took a deep breath
and looked at him imploringly. "Well—and here you
are, right here, and you look so good, Bertie. I just
changed the sheets this morning and . . . I wish you'd
come, Bertie. It'd be nice, y'know? I'd be real good
to you, and—what the hell, we're all grown up, and
since you're not married now or nothin', how about
it?"

"Why, Esther!" he said, astounded.

She grinned, and flushed a little. "I know. It ain't
exactly *my* style, either, as a matter of fact. But Carl
won't never know the difference. And—it's just for
old times' sake, Bertie. Just to get you outa my
system."

He was touched, and faintly roused, by this ap-
peal. It had been such a long, long time. Maybe it
would be better not to be alone. Just for tonight. He
looked at her, and the eyes looking back at him were
misty and full of memories. But . . . well . . . he
looked at the hand that had reached out to touch
his sleeve. The nails were bitten to the quick, the
knuckles were rumpled and grimy. And all at once
his head was flooded with realities: his own room
at home, his own fresh sheets, the shining silver
backs of his brushes laid just so on his bureau top.
The present flowed in cleanly all around him and he

was Herbert Rowbarge once again. These hands of Esther's on his body—the notion made him shudder, and his headache widened. He pushed away the half-eaten pie. "Esther," he said, "I'm sorry." He heard the coldness in his voice, but—well—that was the way he felt.

She stood up, shoving her chair back sharply. "Yeah. Well. It was just an idea."

"I'm sorry," he said again.

"Forget it. Okay?" she said stiffly. "You always was a jerk, anyways."

He paid his bill quickly and left.

Outside, he searched for a drugstore, found one, and went in. His temples were pounding now, and he wanted a headache powder badly. The druggist leaned across the counter and frowned. "Well!" he said. "You here again? Didn't expect to see *you* again."

"What?" said Herbert.

"Don't tell me," said the druggist. "You've got another headache."

"I've got a headache, yes," said Herbert, surprised. "How did *you* know?"

"You ought to see someone about that," said the druggist, spooning a measure of soft white grains into a glass of water. "Too many headaches could be a sign of something."

"A sign of what?"

"See a doctor," the druggist repeated. "That's my advice."

"I don't get headaches that often," said Herbert defensively.

"Two in a day," said the druggist. "That's too many. Take it from me."

Herbert paused, and then he said, "Oh—I see. You're thinking of somebody else. I've never been in here before."

"It's not smart, putting off the doctor," said the druggist disapprovingly, ignoring this disclaimer. "Pretending it isn't there won't make an illness go away."

Herbert drank down the mixture with a shiver and gave the glass back to the druggist. "How much?" he said.

"Same as before," said the druggist. "Five cents." He squinted reflectively at Herbert. "Eyes can do it, you know," he said.

"Do what?" said Herbert. He was almost beginning to enjoy this conversation.

"Bring on a headache," said the druggist sagely. "You drive clear down from the lake, that could do it. Eyestrain from driving."

"The lake?" said Herbert, taken aback.

"Lake *Erie*," said the druggist. He leaned across the counter again and peered at Herbert closely. "Didn't you say you're from Sandusky? Say, are you all right?"

Herbert threw up his hands helplessly and laughed. "I'm not from Sandusky," he said. "I'm from Mussel Point. You've got me mixed up with someone else, I tell you. I've never been in here before."

"Okay, okay, suit yourself," said the druggist with a shrug.

Herbert left a nickel on the counter and went to the door. "See a doctor," the druggist called after him, "and stay off the roads."

There was still a little daylight left, and Herbert stood on the sidewalk wondering what to do with it. Maybe he should motor out there now, to the Home, and take a look at it. Or—get it over with; go in and talk to Mrs. Frate. Mrs. Frate? My God, she wouldn't still be there. Someone else would have taken over. Still—well—all right. He would do it now. Why not?

The Lincoln consumed the single mile too easily. Arriving before he was ready at the foot of the hill where the Home stood, Herbert braked and pulled the car over to the side of the road. Well, there it was. The long, upcurving driveway, the three tall pines, the heavy, solid old building, its gray stone almost blue in the twilight. The best Home in the state, they'd often been told, and now, staring at it, Herbert thought to himself that it wasn't a bad-looking building; in some ways it looked like a mansion, with its wide veranda and commanding gaze across the valley. But it wasn't a mansion. It was a Home.

He noticed, then, a car in the driveway, parked at the steps leading up to the veranda—a big blue

Buick. The Buick was as new and shiny as his Lincoln; in the half-light, its chromium gleamed. Well, probably just someone leaving off a box of toys or something. Still, the Buick disturbed him. I'd look like a damned fool barging in there now, he thought. I'll wait till they go away.

There was no other sign of life. No lights yet in the windows, no sound of children's voices. Without the Buick, the whole sweep of hill and buildings would have looked abandoned. He watched it all flatten as the light faded, till at last, through the square of his windshield, it looked like a picture from an album—a picture of some place that was gone now, done with. Like the past. The Home of his fragmentary memories, dim though it was, was clearer in his head than this. For *this* Home he could conjure up no feeling, no stab of recognition. It was nothing but a building on a hill.

It came to him then that he didn't care a straw whose son he was, and never had. Whoever he'd been when he came to the Home, he was someone else now. His gaze roamed the hilltop—the barn, the fields, the old stone building proper—and tried one final time to find a self there, to see and feel it all again. But there was nothing. It must have happened, he supposed, but to some other person. Esther Conkling had kissed a grubby little no one of a child behind the barn, not him. He was a grown man. He was Herbert Rowbarge. He must remember, when he got back, to tell Dick not to call him Bertie any more.

Then, in the stillness, he heard the Home's big door bang shut. The figure of a man in overcoat and hat stood for a moment on the steps, a dark silhouette against the last of the sunset. The figure stood there slumped and thoughtful and, Herbert thought, a little sad. Well, so what—a Home was a sad place. Any Home. At last the figure moved slowly down to the Buick, opened the door, and climbed in. Headlights flared, the car rolled forward down the driveway, its powerful motor droning. The headlights' glare swept into his eyes, blinding him, and he put up his hands to his face. Then, reaching the road, the car turned north, away from him, away from Gaitsburg. Herbert dropped his hands and watched till the red of the taillights disappeared around a curve.

It was gone. He could go in now, if he was ever going to. Well, was he? No. The loneliness of the man on the steps had touched him somehow, reminded him of his own loneliness; and suddenly he wanted badly to leave this dead and disconnected place, leave and go home to Mussel Point, to the Pleasure Dome. Remembering his house, the park, the lions on the merry-go-round, he decided he would go home first thing in the morning—and never leave again.

He started up the Lincoln and switched on the headlights, and at once a sense of now, of life, suffused him. On the dashboard a golden glow sprang up behind the dials. Needles quivered, bright reflections winked on every polished surface, and as he backed the car around, it purred, then roared appreciation as he shifted into gear. Almost happily, he swung into the road, and realized that his headache was gone. He shouldn't have come down to Gaitsburg. It hadn't solved anything at all. But—well—at least it had recalled to him what he was now, and where he belonged. If he was going to give in to the madness, better to do it there. But he didn't feel the madness just now. Instead, he felt strong and solid, sitting behind the wheel. He pressed his foot on the accelerator and the Lincoln leapt forward.

This feeling of solid strength, solid respectability, was good. Into his head came a fragment of something he had read somewhere: "Everyone likes and respects a self-made man." At the thought he laughed aloud. There never was, he said to himself, a man so self-made as me. And, humming, he rolled back into Gaitsburg for the final time.

Wednesday evening, May 28, 1952

Louisa Rowbarge carries the remains of a chocolate cake out to the kitchen. "Dessert was so-o-o good, Fawn," she says to the woman washing dishes at the sink. "And the ham was just perfect."

"I wrapped the rest up careful for your dinner Friday," says Fawn. "I got the day off, y'know."

Louisa nods. "Memorial Day," she says. "Will your family all be together?"

"Yep," says Fawn. "All but Lorraine. She's still down to Zeenie"—by which she means Xenia, some fifty miles south—"on that kidney stone." Lorraine is a practical nurse and is often away on cases, the details of which Fawn bestows on Babe and Louisa at the least sign of encouragement.

"Well, that's nice," says Louisa hastily, hoping to avoid a full report. "I mean, nice to have so many of your children around."

"Yeah, well," says Fawn, and leaves the response,

whatever it might have been, hanging forever un-
finished as she scours away at a big enameled roasting pan. "Mr. Rowbarge gone back over to the park?"

"No," says Louisa. "As a matter of fact, he went to
bed. He said he was feeling tired."

"Tired!" Fawn exclaims. "I should think so! At his
age, he oughta be rockin' in the sun with his memories 'steada push push push the way he does."

"I know," says Louisa. "We're kind of worried
about him."

"Ain't like him to go to bed directly he's had his
dinner," Fawn observes.

"No," says Louisa. "I was going to call Babe and
see if she wanted to go to the movies, but I hate to
leave him."

"The movies!" says Fawn. "You two sure do like to
waste time. What's playin'?"

"It's called *He Ran All the Way*," says Louisa.
"John Garfield's in it."

Fawn curls her lip. "Sounds like a loser to me,"
she says.

Louisa sighs. "Well, I don't want to leave Daddy
anyway. Not when he isn't feeling well."

"That's right," says Fawn. "Get outa the way while
I mop up the counters. I gotta get on home."

Louisa goes to the living room and stares out the
window. The light is fading, but now, with the trees
in leaf, sunsets reflected in the lake beyond the road
are hidden from view. There is nothing to look at
through the glass but a neighbor's cat, a gray tom,
who is crossing the lawn with something small,

limp, and furry dangling from his jaws. Louisa says, "Oh, dear," and raps on the window with her knuckles. The cat pauses, looking toward the house, and then, with princely indifference, glides on and disappears under the shrubbery.

At the same time Fawn comes down the hall, her pocketbook under her arm, and says, "Was that you knockin'?"

"Yes," says Louisa. "That terrible cat from down the road—he's killed something again. It's a wonder there's a chipmunk or a field mouse left anywhere around."

"That's the way they do," says Fawn. "Can't change it."

"I know," says Louisa sadly.

"Cheer up," says Fawn. "You ain't a chipmunk." And then she says, "What's the matter? You look kinda mossy."

"Oh, I don't know," says Louisa, embarrassed, though she is grateful, too, for this attention. Fawn can be gentle and motherly on rare occasions, making of the slim ten years between their ages a span that is at once far wider and more bridgeable, and Louisa finds it soothing, hopes for it, even. "I guess I've got spring fever," she says. "I just wish . . . something would *happen*. Nothing ever happens."

Fawn says, "Go down and hang around the road. Maybe some lowlife'll jump ya from the bushes."

"Good grief, Fawn," says Louisa, laughing. "I don't want *that* kind of excitement."

"Oh, no?" says Fawn cryptically. "Well, I gotta go."

She tucks her pocketbook firmly between her knees, and taking from the hall closet an aged jacket of red and white sateen with *Mussel Point Marauders* spelled out in felt letters on the back, she shrugs into it. "Why doncha ring up your sister, get her to come play cards over here or somethin'?" she suggests over her shoulder, zipping up the jacket. She zips with care, for the jacket is a treasured relic from the glory days of her youngest son, Sam, a basketball star in high school fifteen years before.

"Well," says Louisa, "I would, but she's probably tired out. Aunt Opal had bridge over there this afternoon, and Babe spent all day getting ready."

"Oh," says Fawn, retrieving the pocketbook. "Had enough cards for one day, huh."

"Yes, probably so. And anyway, I'm just too restless to sit still."

Fawn says, reasonably, "You was gonna sit still in a movie house."

"That's different," says Louisa.

Fawn gives it up. "Well," she says briskly, "I got things to do. See ya tomorrow." And she is gone down the hall and out the kitchen door.

Louisa drops down on the sofa. The living room glows with the dim golden light that defines May evenings so sweetly, while outside, birdsong soars and trembles from the trees along the road. "I wish . . ." she says to herself, but cannot finish the thought. Her head fills with visions from movies she has seen where heroines have loved, lost, triumphed, died, been swept away on horseback or stowed away on ships. *The Sea Wolf*, starring John Garfield. "We saw that on our thirty-fourth birthday," she thinks, and then, as scenes from the movie wash across her memory, she murmurs, "Oh, I wish I was Ida Lupino!" Then, sprawled on the cushions of the sofa, she drowses in the growing dark and dreams of things happening, formless but thrilling things, where she is Ida and John is John, and the sea is all around them, sweeping them away.

September 1941

Herbert Rowbarge walked alone up Lake Street in the cool autumn dark. It was good to be out in the quiet of the town after all that babble at dinner, good to have the birthday party over with at last, his duty done. For Opal had said, "Surely you're not going to disappoint the girls and just do *nothing!*"

"They're hardly girls anymore," he had answered testily. "They're full-grown women, Opal."

"Well, so what if they are?" she had demanded. "Since when did a full-grown woman not want a birthday party? And anyway, they'll always seem like girls to me."

"Well, they're not," he had said, "though I grant you they act like it. They're going to be thirty-six years old."

"Thirty-*four*, Herbert," said Opal. "Good grief, you really take the cake."

"Oh!" he had said. "Thirty-*four*! Well. That's different. Why, they've got *years* of childhood left. Forgive me—I didn't realize."

But Opal was immune to his sarcasm. "You can give them a dinner at the Inn," she had said firmly. "Just for the three of you, and Stuart, Walter, and me. No point getting all the Festeens involved."

And it had been all right, he supposed, except for the talk about war. Opal and Stuart argued all the time these days about war, and it was boring, a waste of time. For once, Stuart was right—even that idiot Roosevelt wasn't so dumb as to get us involved all over again. But aside from that, the dinner had been all right. The steaks were overdone, but the Inn had produced a nice cake with candles, and the twins had been happy. He had given them a generous check—though Opal had frowned and said, "One check? You've got two separate daughters, you know"—and Opal and Stuart had given them matching white sweaters of some fuzzy sort of stuff. And Walter—Walter had given each of them a bookend. That Walter! He was something. The bookends were very handsome—heavy brass, and expensive—but in the shape of two sheep, and they were wrapped one for each. It was, on the surface of it, a nice present, but it was funny, too. Subtle. Especially in light of the fuzzy sweaters. The girls hadn't caught it, of course. They'd pronounced the sheep "darling." Herbert shook his head. That Walter! And then Babe and Louisa had gone off in the Lincoln to a movie in Bell Fountain. He had refused to go along, and had refused, too, a lift from the Looses back to the house. He wanted to walk, he told Opal; he needed the exercise.

But it wasn't that at all. What he needed was to go, alone, to the park and see how things were. He and Walter had closed it for the season a week ago, but that was just it—he and *Walter* had closed it. Walter was doing a first-rate job, but he was always *there*. Herbert wanted to have it to himself for a while. But he hadn't said so at dinner. It sounded kind of silly. Still, he had stowed a flashlight in his overcoat pocket, and had looked forward all day to this solitary visit.

There was almost no one about on Lake Street. The souvenir stands were boarded up, the dance hall dark, the park behind its high board fence a pool of silence. Herbert knew that once he was inside he could bring it all back in an instant to the blaze of light and music that defined it all summer. All he had to do was throw the levers in the powerhouse. But he didn't want to. He liked it like this, dreaming in a sort of hibernation. It made him feel protective, and paternal.

He went past the padlocked main gates and around the corner, following the fence along the edge of the empty parking lot. And then, coming to the work gate, he took a bunch of keys from his pocket, let himself in, and locked the gate again behind him. Good. Charlie, the night watchman, wasn't anywhere in sight. But there was a single red bulb set high on a pole near the gate and Herbert switched it on. It was a signal light, to let the watchman know that he was there; a precaution, and a wise one, for Charlie carried a pistol.

Against the pale night sky, Herbert's great machines loomed shadowy and motionless around him, their steel frames glinting, their various cars and controls bedded down for the winter in heavy canvas shrouds. Shutters on game booths were bolted into place, the pavilion bare of benches and tables, the lake beyond it black and slick and still. The ticket booths were containers of a darker dark, each a Cyclops with its round eye of glass, each eye with a blacker pupil where the glass was cut away to take in money and dispense little passports of cardboard.

His heart lifting, Herbert moved among his sleeping monsters quietly toward the center of the park, where the boardwalk divided to curve around the wide circle occupied by the merry-go-round. Here there were permanent benches of concrete and wood arranged so that people could keep an eye on the children as they rode, and Herbert sat down on one, drawing his overcoat closer around him in a sudden rise of wind. He stayed for a long time looking at the merry-go-round, not thinking of anything at all, conscious only of warm, almost physical pleasure.

The animals were wrapped in canvas, but Herbert

knew exactly where the lions were. All around the edge of the roof were carved wooden cupids playing instruments, and the one above the lions, as if to celebrate their presence, was blowing a long gold horn. It was directly in front of him. "Tan-ta-*rah*," he whispered, and flushed at once, looking quickly around to see if the watchman was near. But he was still alone. He stood up, feeling foolish but happy, and went on in the dark toward the front of the park.

At the Penny Arcade he paused and looked in at the banks of games, dim in the feeble glow of a work light hung from a central rafter. The Arcade was not yet boarded up, for a man was coming in the morning to repair a few machines lamed by the summer's exertions. Herbert didn't like the Arcade. It was—unbeautiful. But people expected there to be one, and it had paid for itself more than twenty times over since its installation. He stood there frowning at it just the same, and then his eye fell on the polished glass dome of the mechanical gypsy fortune-teller.

She was gazing at him through the glass, her head tilted to one side, her long-fingered hands poised over a row of tarot cards laid out on the narrow shelf behind which she must sit forever. She looked surprisingly real with her eyes turned on him, her painted lips parted, the gold coins hanging from her headdress and ears the faintest sparkle in the gloom of her enclosure. Herbert took a nickel from his pocket and, crossing over to her, dropped the nickel into the slot and pulled a waiting knob.

Abruptly the gypsy began to move. Her hands jerked back and forth over the cards, her head turned from side to side, the gold coins trembling. Then it was over. She gazed at him again, motionless, and, looking down, he pulled out the square of white cardboard that presented itself from a slot of its own, and tried to decipher the words printed on it. But for this the darkness was too thick. He took the flashlight from his pocket and switched it on, focusing its bright circle on the card, and read: *The loss which is unknown is no loss at all.*

He stared at the words, his contentment swept away by a flood of desolation. Against it, he said aloud, roughly, "Where does Walter get this stuff?" And then, sensing a movement, he raised his head to the face of the fortune-teller and saw, instead, reflected in the glass, his own face, grotesque in the underlighting of the flashlight in his hand. At once he felt the dreaded twinkling down his spine. He dropped the fortune card and, fumbling with the flashlight, managed at last to switch it off. The dark returned in a rush, his reflection vanished. The eyes of the mechanical gypsy gazed again into his. He wanted, suddenly, to smash the glass dome, to wrench the gypsy from her moorings. Instead, he said to himself, "You're a fool." He squared his shoulders and returned the flashlight to his pocket, thinking, "Better go on home now." He turned and left the Arcade and headed back the way he had come.

Again, by the merry-go-round, he stopped, but

could not regain his pleasure in it. He longed to unwrap the shrouded lions, to stroke their manes. They could always ease these freakish moods that rose so abruptly to plague him. But how could he explain such a thing to the watchman? Why, Charlie would think he was crazy. And then the thought re-phrased itself: Charlie would find out he was crazy. He stood quite still, annoyed with himself, sharply aware of the darkness and the silence.

What would it be like, he wondered, to be really crazy? For he wasn't, of course. Not yet, anyway. If you were really crazy, you would lose your *self*; your brain, the lighted part, would slip away, slowly, under the dark part. You would feel it slipping, maybe. Try to clutch at it. But be unable to hold on. Or maybe you wouldn't feel it slipping. Maybe it would simply *go*. Not like a lunar eclipse, gradual, inexorable. More like a spill of ink, a great and total blot. Or a fall, with the snap of something breaking, into a hole without a bottom. And then— but he couldn't quite imagine what would happen next, except that the dark part would be in charge, as it seemed to be in dreams. Maybe it would be nice. Relaxing. Some dreams were nice. But some were horrible. Some sent you rising fast to the sur-face in a sweat, your heart booming like a drum. Except, if you were crazy, you'd never find the surface.

He was roused from these speculations by the watchman, a big, grim-faced man of about his own

age, a retired Bell Fountain policeman. "Evenin',
Mr. Rowbarge, sir," said the watchman. "Glad you're
here. Found a coupla boards bashed out of the fence
back by the beach. Don't know when it happened.
Seen anything suspicious?"

"No," said Herbert.

"Well, I'm lookin' extra careful," said the watchman. "Somebody mighta got in. You goin' home
now?"

"In a few minutes," said Herbert.

"Well, if you see anything, don't sing out. Come
and get me. I'll be up doin' the buildings in front."

"All right," said Herbert. "Good night, Charlie."

The watchman disappeared and Herbert moved on
down the boardwalk. He walked firmly, feeling better,
and was nearly to the work gate when all at once a
roll of thunder shook the sky, and as if a hose had
been trained on the park, it began to rain—hard
rain, cold and driving. Turning up his collar, he
wheeled about, looking for shelter, and saw nearby
the ticket booth that stood by the shrouded Bullet. He
ran to it, groping in his pocket for his keys, saw that
its little door was ajar, and, pulling it open, ducked
inside. He yanked it shut behind him, turned, fumbling for the stool he knew should be there, and
tripped against something large and soft. At the
same moment a hoarse voice cried plaintively from
the floor, "Hey, watch wha'cher doin'!"

Herbert stiffened and, as well as he could in the
limited space, moved back, flattening himself against

the door. "Who are you?" he said, finding his voice. "What do you think you're doing in here?" He reached into his pocket, brought out the flashlight, and, switching it on, turned the beam on the figure at his feet. But he saw only a bundle of dark clothing, arms wrapped around the head, the knees drawn up. "How'd you get in here, anyway?" he said unsteadily. He reached behind him with his free hand to open the door, found the knob and turned it, but he had slammed it too hard. It was jammed.

"Shut that durn thing off," the voice demanded.

"I certainly will not," said Herbert. "Get up from there."

"Now jus' a minute," said the voice. "I wuz here firs', y'know. Who the hell are *you*, tellin' me what t'do?" The flashlight was abruptly, powerfully, snatched from Herbert's grasp, the beam turned back on its owner. There was a moment of silence then, while Herbert, eyes squeezed shut, pushed at the door behind his back. At last the voice said, "*Uh*-oh. If it ain't Schwimmbeck. Didn' figure on ya follerin' me *this* far."

Schwimmbeck? Herbert turned his head away from the glare and said, "My name isn't Schwimm-beck," and added, "Give me that flashlight."

"No, don't think so," said the voice. "Might come in handy." The light switched off suddenly and the booth went black, much blacker, it seemed, than before, and smaller, tighter, full of breathing. At last the voice, utterly disembodied, said, "Lissen, if

ya follered me all the way down from Sandusky, ya
mus' be hurtin' for that twenny. Jeez, I'm real sorry,
Schwimmbeck, but I drunk it all up."

"What?" said Herbert, his heart pounding.
"What?"

"Jus' you and me shut up in here," said the voice.
"Rainin' like bejeezus, no one else around, might
as well have a little talk." It sighed, and then
turned plaintive again. "It ain't as if ya couldn' spare
a twenny, big shot like you. Maybe if I'd ast ya,
you'da give it to me, huh, Schwimmbeck. Sure you
would—like hell. Tha's how you big shots stay big,
ain't it? Don't never let go a nuthin'.."

"What in God's name are you talking about?" said
Herbert. "My name isn't Schwimmbeck." Alarmed,
and a little dizzy, he pushed hard at the door, but it
stuck firm. "My God," he thought wildly, "I'm trapped
in here with . . . something terrible!" There was a
bumping sound and suddenly he felt a heavy body,
upright, leaning against him, and smelled sour
breath on his face. "Get away from me!" he cried.
"Who *are* you?"

At first there was no answer—just the breath on
his face and the hard rattle of rain on the thin roof
of the booth, the sheeting of rain down the sides of
the booth, closing him in. And then the voice, close
to his ear, said, "Man t' man, Schwimmbeck, ya gotta
admit I did my job, kep' your damn movie house all
swep' out, worked my tail off. Only took a twenny."
It laughed loosely, directly in his ear. "Lissen,
Schwimmbeck, you got a brother? *I* do. Ain't seen

'im in a coon's age. Never was no good, jus' a lousy
bum. Had a twenny once, he took it offa me slick as
a whistle. Cut 'im up with a butcher knife." The
voice laughed again, its breath foul on Herbert's
cheek. "Got a butcher knife on ya, Schwimmbeck?
Won't do ya no good, 'cause I ain't got yer damn
twenny anyways. Drunk it all up."

Herbert pushed again on the door, to no avail,
dread thickening in his stomach. "My name isn't
Schwimmbeck!" he cried. "It's Rowbarge!"

"Lookit," said the voice disgustedly. "I may not be
a big shot like you, but that don't mean I'm stupid.
Know somethin', Schwimmbeck? I don't like you.
Never did."

"Get away," said Herbert. But the heavy body
pressed on him, so that he could barely move. The
ticket booth seemed to have tipped off the world and
gone plummeting into an emptiness where there was
nothing but rushing black air and rain, and he knew
that without the wall to lean on, he'd have slid to a
heap on the floor. This was what it was like. A slipping away of self. A fall into a hole without a bottom.
"My name isn't Schwimmbeck, I tell you," he said
again, uselessly.

The flashlight flared full in his face, and then
switched off. "Yer a liar, Schwimmbeck," said the
voice softly.

Herbert trembled, something seemed to crack in-
side his head, releasing a fog of panic. "I'm not
Schwimmbeck!" he insisted. "I'm Herbert Rowbarge!"
But, with the fog, a terrifying doubt engulfed him.

Why, there had been a time, he knew, when he'd had no name, been no one at all. His blood seemed to drain into his ankles and feet, and he feared he would faint. Instead, to his horror, his face, all on its own, crumpled, and tears stung his eyes. "I'm Herbert Rowbarge," he whispered, but he felt that it was a lie. There was no Herbert Rowbarge. There was only this voice with its judgments—and Schwimmbeck. His breath caught, and the tears rolled down his cheeks.

The voice said in his ear, still softly, "Gotcher wallet on ya, Schwimmbeck?"

Herbert made a last violent effort to open the door, driving his buttocks and shoulders hard against it, and at the same moment sensed that the flashlight had been lifted and was coming down fast toward his head. As he thrust backward, he ducked, and they both crashed against the door. It sprang open and Herbert fell out into the rain, fell hard onto the flooded boardwalk, and the body with the voice fell with him, sprawling across his legs. "Charlie!" Herbert yelled, struggling to free himself. *"Charlie!"*

The body became a man who drew his breath in sharply and rolled off to one side, scrabbling to hands and knees. *"Charlie!"* yelled Herbert again, while the man paused spiderlike above him.

Footsteps pounded toward them down the boardwalk, the beam of a powerful lantern swept over them. The man crouched for another instant and then got up and ran, a flapping mass of arms and clothing. "Shoot him, Charlie! *Shoot him!*" screamed

Herbert. The gun went off with a deafening *crack* and Herbert, sitting up, ears ringing, was swept with savage pleasure. His lips stretched back tight across his teeth in a crazy grin, and he crowed, "Is he dead? Did you kill him, Charlie?"

"Not even sure I hit 'im," said the watchman. "You okay, Mr. Rowbarge?"

"I'm all right!" Herbert cried, faint with relief to hear his name. "I'm all *right*! He thought I was someone else. And then he tried to hit me with my flashlight!"

"Well," said the watchman, swinging the lantern's beam to the boardwalk ahead, "never mind. Looks like we got 'im."

"We got 'im," Herbert echoed giddily. "He kept calling me Schwimmbeck. But we got 'im."

The watchman helped Herbert to his feet and then went forward through the rain and bent to look at the man lying tumbled and still on the boardwalk. "Can't tell if he's dead or not," he reported, coming back. "I gotta go call the police."

"All right," said Herbert. He was still grinning crazily, his voice too loud in the hush. "I'll turn the lights on." He went off carefully, stepping wide around the body of the man, to the powerhouse by the work gate. Here, unlocking the door, he reached into the blackness and found, unerringly, the proper lever. He pulled it and at once, like a great eye blinking open, the park awoke with a blaze of ten thousand colored bulbs, dazzling, glorious, throwing back reflections from every pool and puddle, brilliant through the haze of rain like fireworks caught and frozen in a burst of rushing stars. Herbert, in the door of the powerhouse, gazed up, his heart racing, and tried to catch his breath. He felt triumphant, exultant, swollen with self. He was Herbert Rowbarge, risen, and the park was his again.

Thursday, May 29, 1952

Babe Rowbarge, in robe and slippers, basks in a broad beam of morning sun that has spilled into Aunt Opal's living room and made itself warmly at home across the sofa, the polished coffee table, a fortunate section of carpet. It is only eight o'clock, but Aunt Opal has left the house already for a shopping trip to Cleveland with her Wednesday bridge friends—a plan hatched the afternoon before over Babe's fruit-betty bars and tea. And now Babe has the whole long day entirely to herself. She sips at a cup of coffee luxuriously and opens the Mussel Point *Courier*, a twice-a-week paper flung at the doorstep in the dawns of every Monday and Thursday by a pimpled presence seen only once a month on collection day. This presence was, a few years past, Carmichael Bray, the minister's son. Now it is someone less notorious.

Yawning, Babe wriggles her toes inside the fuzz

of her slippers and blinks at the banner headline, HERE WE GO AGAIN, under which is spread, in slightly smaller letters: PLEASURE DOME TO OPEN TOMORROW. The entire front page is a happy collection of items all reporting on the season to come. "NEW RIDE A SURE BET AT THE PARK. Tomorrow at 10 a.m. Mr. Herbert Rowbarge will christen a Tunnel of Love, the latest in a long succession of . . ." "MEMORIAL DAY VISITORS TO HEAR HIGH SCHOOL BAND. An exciting program of marching music has been . . ." "BINGO GAMES TO BE EXTENDED. This summer, according to the Recreation Committee, Post 2832 of the VFW will open its doors on Friday evenings in addition to . . ." "LIFEGUARD OFFERS SWIMMING LESSONS. Tuesday mornings will again be reserved for children between the ages of . . ."

"How nice," thinks Babe. "How nice and normal and . . . and *annual!*"

Precisely at this moment, the telephone rings. The ring is the same as always—a sharp, shrill intrusion. But afterward Babe will claim that she knew at once from the sound of it what had happened—that it sounded, this time, entirely different and made her heart jump right into her mouth.

She leaps up, letting the *Courier* slide to the floor, and hurries out to the hall where the telephone stands on a small table just below a mirror. She picks up the receiver and says, "Hello?"

"Babe," says a breathless voice, "it's Louisa. Dr. Herdman's here—Daddy collapsed."

"Collapsed!"

"Yes. Walter came for breakfast and we were eating and everything was fine, and then Daddy just—blacked out."

"Oh, my God," says Babe.

"I called Dr. Herdman and he came right away. He and Walter got Daddy upstairs and he's with him now and—oh, Babe, Walter thought it might be a *heart* attack, just like Uncle Stuart."

"Oh, Louisa, no."

"Walter thought—hold on, Babe. Can you hold on? Dr. Herdman's coming down. I'll go see what he says."

Babe stands rigid, the receiver pressed hard to her ear, and stares at her reflection in the mirror. Hair frowsy, face bare of makeup, the woman in the mirror looks like no one Babe has ever seen before. She strains to make out the distant, low patter of voices, and then jumps as Louisa's voice comes suddenly loud over the wire. "Babe—are you still there?"

"Of course I'm still here!" she says sharply. "What did he say?"

"It's not a heart attack," Louisa reports. "Dr. Herdman says it's just a little stroke."

"A *little* stroke?"

"That's what he said. It's got a complicated name, something about transient—wait a minute. What, Walter? Oh. Yes. Transient ischaemic episodes, Babe. Little strokes. He gave Daddy some medicine and he says he'll probably be all right as long as he stays in bed."

"Oh, my God," says Babe. "A stroke."

"But just a little one," says Louisa. "He's not paralyzed or anything, and he won't have to—hold on a minute, Babe."

This time the interval is longer. Babe waits, staring at herself in the mirror. She is suddenly deeply self-conscious. No one should be allowed to look at you when you're getting news like this, she thinks. Abruptly she turns her back on her reflection and stares instead into the living room. The pages of the *Courier* lie open on the floor and from where she is standing she can see that Ellison's Drug Store is having a sale. *LAST DAY MADNESS!* the ad cries happily. *COTTON BALLS—100 boxed—29¢. TOILET TISSUE—double roll—23¢. WHILE THEY LAST—Hairbrush and comb set—only . . .*

"Babe, I'm sorry to keep you waiting so long." Louisa's voice seems to roar, and again Babe jumps. "Dr. Herdman just left. He says we have to keep Daddy in bed for a while. He gave him a shot and he has to take a pill once a day."

"But, Louisa," says Babe, "how *is* he? I mean, will he be all right? Does he feel awful?"

"That's the thing," says Louisa. "He evidently feels perfectly fine, now. Or that's what he told Dr. Herdman. It's going to be hell on wheels keeping him in bed. Especially tomorrow! Oh, Babe, I just know he's going to want to go down to the park for the opening."

Babe turns resolutely back to face the mirror.

"Louisa," she says, "I'm coming over. I'll help you sit on him."

"Well, all right," says Louisa, "but not to *stay*. He wouldn't want that. But come on over later and look in on him. Maybe the three of us—I mean, Walter and us—can make him see he's got to stay quiet."

"Yes," says Babe. "I'll be there in an hour." She hangs up the phone and goes to stand in the middle of the living room, pulling her bathrobe closer over her chest. She feels cold, her feet and hands are freezing. The angle of the sunbeam has shortened now, and glares on the surface of the coffee table, revealing small imperfections in the varnish and a faint coating of dust. Babe thinks, "I'd better clean up," but she continues to stand there. Never in the five years of their separation has she missed Louisa so much, or felt so solitary, so full of the wonder of death. The thought occurs to her that maybe, much sooner than they had supposed, she and Louisa can be together again. Shamed, she pushes the thought away, but it lights the back of her mind and she finds herself saying, in a whisper, "He never gave a damn about us."

Her shame deepens, and, in penance, she begins to bustle: collects and folds the scattered sheets of the *Courier*, carries her cup to the kitchen, returns with a cloth to wipe the dust from the coffee table. By nine o'clock she has cleaned up the breakfast dishes, made the beds, scoured Aunt Opal's bathroom and her own, and is dressed and ready. It has been a long time since the three of them, she and Louisa and Daddy, were alone together. They will be that way more now, she decides as she leaves the house. Five years is long enough.

January 1947

Herbert Rowbarge took off his overcoat and hat and put them away in the closet, and then he sat down on the staircase and yanked at his overshoes. Terrible day for a funeral, he thought to himself as he struggled with the clinging rubber. Well, poor old Stuart, he hadn't exactly had much to say about it. Funny when a doctor died. You'd think they'd know a way around it.

He stood up at last, overshoes in hand, and wondered what to do with them. They glistened with rain, and the soles were caked with mud. "No one has ever," he said aloud, "solved the problem of what to do with overshoes."

Babe—or was it Louisa?—came down the hall from the kitchen, carrying a tray laden with tea things. "Did you say something, Daddy?" she asked. Her nose and eyes were red from weeping, and he hated that. He scowled at her.

"I *said*," he repeated, "I never know what to do with overshoes."

"Oh, here, Daddy, I'll take them. They ought to be cleaned off."

"I'll do it," said Louisa—or was it Babe?—from the living room. "You go ahead and pour the tea, Babe." Oh. So this *was* Babe with the tray. Good. He'd been right for once.

He went into the living room and sat down in his armchair, stretching out his long legs with a groan. It was no good, at his age, standing around in graveyards in this kind of weather. Sixty-seven! He sighed, leaned his head back, and closed his eyes. Well, well, old Stuart. Still, he'd had his threescore ten and then some; and a heart attack—well, it wasn't such a bad way to go. Quick, anyway. Opal was taking it well, and so was Walter. Of course, Walter was almost more *his* son than Stuart's; had been ever since he came on at the park. Families! Oh my, families.

"Here's your tea, Daddy. Is it strong enough?"

He opened his eyes and looked at the offered cup. "It's all right."

"I can make it stronger if you want me to."

"No, no, it's all right. Just put it down."

"I put the sugar in for you."

"All right."

"Would you like a cookie?"

"No."

"They're the kind you like. With raisins."

"*No!* Thank you. No cookie." Silly word, cookie, for a grown man to have to say.

Louisa came in, then, with a spotless overshoe dangling from each hand. "How's this, Daddy? Don't they look like new?"

"They *are* new," he said. "I just bought them yesterday. They're only overshoes. Nothing to gush over."

"But I only meant—"

"I know. Yes. Thanks for cleaning them off. I appreciate it."

"Shall I put them in the closet?"

He took a sip of tea and tried to swallow down his rising irritation. "Yes, Babe."

"Louisa, Daddy."

"All right, yes, *Louisa*. Put them in the closet." My God, where else?

Louisa laid the overshoes on the closet floor and came back into the living room. "Are you ready for more tea, Daddy?" she asked him.

"No—no, thank you."

"You're not having a cookie."

"I don't *want* a cookie."

"Oh. All right. Are you sure? They're your favorite kind, with raisins."

"I've thought it over carefully," he said, "and my decision is final. I hope you'll be able to live with it."

"Oh, Daddy," said Louisa.

"I already offered him one," said Babe. "He isn't hungry."

"Oh," said Louisa. She sat down on the sofa next

to Babe and for a while they sipped in silence. Herbert looked at them over the rim of his cup. My God. Were any two people ever so exactly alike?

"You two are forty years old," he said.

"Next September, Daddy," they answered in one voice, then looked at each other and smiled.

Damn them, he thought resentfully. They were so damned smug. He said, aloud, "It seems to me you're old enough to stop dressing alike. Don't you think so?"

"We've always dressed alike," said Babe. "What's wrong with it?"

"It's fun," said Louisa.

"Fun!" he snorted. "Well, I'll tell you what it is for *me*. It's damned confusing, that's what it is. It makes me nervous." He set down his cup with a clatter and stood up, glaring at them. My God, he thought, they look like two crows on a fence.

"Anyway," said Louisa, "we had to wear black dresses to the funeral, you know, and black dresses all look exactly alike whether they are or not. Do you want some more tea, Daddy?"

"No," he said. "I'm going upstairs and lie down."

"That's a good idea," said Babe. "You look a little tired. It's been a hard day for all of us."

But he didn't feel tired, exactly. Just restless, and cross. Upstairs in his room, he wandered to the window. It was only four-thirty, but already the light was fading, and the stretch of brown lawn below, the birdbath, the pair of concrete benches, looked blurred and crooked through the rain-streaked panes. And then something intruded itself subtly between him and the wet world outside, and he was suddenly aware of his reflection, dim and ghostly, looking in at him, as if it were another Herbert hanging in the air beyond the glass. He seized the dangling pull of the window shade and jerked it down, shutting out the sight, and crossed to the bed. Here he took off his shoes and socks and sat for a moment, looking down at his feet.

It was nice that there were two of them instead of one, like Dick. He wiggled his toes and decided that in a way his feet looked like two white doves turned backward, his toes the spreading fans of their tails. Things in twos—that was the ticket. Except for daughters. He wondered guiltily why two daughters made him feel so angry. He could hear them talking downstairs, their voices low and intimate. Damn them. They drove him crazy.

Then, as he sat there, he felt a funny, silent *ping* inside his brain, and at once he felt dizzy and confused. "My God, I'm going to faint!" he thought, alarmed. He stood up unsteadily and crossed again to the window as the room rocked around him. Snapping up the shade, lifting the sash, he leaned on the sill and thrust his head out into the rain. The smell of wet leaves, the cold freshness of the air, cleared his vision, and at once he felt better. He drew in his head and shut the window, and again his dim reflection hung there, staring in at him. This time, staring

back, he said, aloud, "No, you can't come in." And
with a short laugh he turned, crossed once more to
the bed, lay down, and was soon fast asleep.

When he woke, an hour had passed and he felt re-
freshed and happy. What was it he'd been thinking
of in that long, delicious moment before he'd dropped
off? Something had eased the tension in his stomach,
some very good idea. Well, it would come back to
him. He climbed out of bed, went once more to the
window, and opened it. The rain had stopped, and
the clouds, thinning, fanned a broad pink smear low
across the sky. Far off around the curve of the lake,
above the leafless trees, he could just see the top, the
highest point, of the roller coaster black against the
sunset. His feeling of happiness deepened, and he
smiled. "I'll go down there tomorrow and see how
the merry-go-round is doing," he thought. It was a
new one, new materials developed during the war.
The lions were the best he'd ever seen.

Changing his clothes for dinner, he put away the
black necktie he'd worn to Stuart's funeral, and that
was when he remembered. Opal. Yes, that was it.
That was the good idea he'd thought of. And now
that he was fully awake, he saw just how good it
was. Opal. It solved everything.

At dinner he said, "Girls, I've decided we need to
spread the riches around a little. Now that Stuart's
dead, your Aunt Opal's going to be lonely."

"Yes, she will," said Babe—or was it Louisa? "We

were talking about that. Walter's with you all day at the park and off in his own place at night, and it's going to be hard for Aunt Opal, being by herself."

The twins looked at each other then, and one of them nodded encouragingly. The other leaned toward Herbert, paused, and said, "Daddy, it looks like we've all been thinking the same thing. We've got so much room here—let's ask Aunt Opal to move in with us. She can be an awful pill sometimes, but still, she's Mother's sister, and we shouldn't just let her sit there all alone."

Herbert twirled the stem of his water glass, pretending to think it over, and then he said, "Well, that would be nice for *us*, but what would Opal do with all her things? All those doodads and pictures and so on? She's pretty attached to that mess she's accumulated. I don't think she'd want to leave her own house. No, what *I* was thinking was that one of you should move in with *her*."

They stared at him blankly. And then: "Move in with *her*? *One* of us?"

"Why, yes," he said, "unless you both want to go, and leave *me* all alone."

"Oh, no, Daddy. But—well—we've never been apart before."

"Well, but don't you think you could handle it," he said, "now that you're all grown up? It's not as if you were *Siamese* twins, you know."

Again they were silent.

"Look," he said, "it wouldn't be forever. We'll try it for a month or two. See how Opal likes it."

"But which one of us? How will we decide which one of us?"

"Well, now, I can't see that it matters, particularly. Switch off every month, take turns. That way," he added, beaming at them paternally, "I wouldn't have to give up either one of you."

"Maybe she won't want us," Babe said hopefully.

"Nonsense," he said. "You said yourselves she's going to be lonely." And then he added, skillfully, "I can't help but think it's what your mother would have wanted."

From this, there could be no recourse.

Opal did like it. Once again there was someone to beat at backgammon, someone to go to the dry cleaner's, someone to boss around as she'd always bossed Stuart and couldn't boss Walter. Someone to talk to on "women's problems," too, someone to rub her back. The arrangement stretched out into the summer, into another summer, into years. Babe and Louisa were together at family dinners, they often met in town. And most days they talked on the telephone. But they were not together. It was an agony, but how could they be so selfish as to think only of themselves? Daddy seemed content, and on top of everything else, below and around and through everything else, was what he'd said, what they deeply believed was true: it was what their mother would have wanted.

Memorial Day, 1952

"Hello?"

"Babe, it's Louisa. You'd better come over. Right away."

"Oh, God, what's happened?"

"It's Daddy. He's gone. Oh, I just *knew* this would happen!"

"What do you mean, 'gone'? Is he—dead?"

"Oh! *No*, Babe, I mean he isn't here! I'd just got him settled down after breakfast—you know, changed his sheets, plumped up the pillows—and I brought the tray downstairs and did his dishes, and then I took the sheets down to the basement and put them in the washer, and when I was coming back up to the kitchen, I heard the car. Babe, he was backing out the car! I ran out to stop him, but it was too late. Oh, Babe, he's gone down to the park. I just know it!"

"He's *driving*?"

"Yes!"

"How could he think of driving, when he isn't even supposed to be out of bed?"

"I don't know."

"Louisa, I'll get Aunt Opal's car and be there in five minutes. We'll go after him. Wait for me in the road."

"All right. But *hurry*!"

"Go on outside. I'll be there right away."

"All right. Goodbye."

"Goodbye."

Memorial Day, 1952

Herbert Rowbarge sits hunched in his bedroom chair, watching while Louisa changes the sheets. She isn't nearly as good at it as the girl, but the girl always gets holidays off, no matter what. They don't care about you, servants. He supposes the girl—what is her name?—he can't in the least remember, but it doesn't matter anyway, they come and go—he supposes the girl will be spending the day at the park, like everybody else. He wants to yell at Louisa to get the blanket straight, he hates it when the blanket isn't straight, but he holds himself quiet and glances at the clock on the bureau. My God, almost a quarter after nine. And the christening begins at ten.

"That's good enough," he says to Louisa. "I want to get in now. I'm tired."

"All right, Daddy. There, it's done. Here—let me help you."

"Get away from me!" he says. "I can get into bed by myself."

He manages it, and she pulls the covers up over him, standing there for a moment afterward, looking down at him with a worried expression. Damn, he says to himself, the blanket's crooked. Aloud he says, "Well, what are you standing there for? How can I get any sleep if you *stand* there like that?"

Louisa picks up the breakfast tray and carries it to the door. "Have a nice nap, Daddy," she says softly.

He waits until he hears her footsteps going down the stairs, and then he throws back the covers and climbs out of bed. Upright, he pauses to see how he feels. Um. A little dizzy, maybe, but all right. Really all right. Idiot doctor! Now to get dressed and get down to the park. There's never been a Memorial Day without him, never a new ride christened without him, and there isn't going to be one now. He goes into his bathroom and takes his razor and soap out of the medicine chest, and then, closing its mirrored door, he peers at his chin. "Maybe I don't have to shave," he thinks. "There isn't much time." He rubs a palm across one cheek to test the bristles, and then he catches the eye of his reflection. A powerful rushing sensation down his spine makes him clutch the basin with both hands, and then, oddly, he feels relaxed and swimmy. He smiles at the pale old man in the mirror, and the pale old man smiles back. "I don't think we have to shave," he says aloud. "Do you?" His voice seems to come from somewhere outside himself, somewhere far away. "Come on, let's get dressed. Let's put our clothes on and get going."

In the bedroom again, he drops his pajamas to the floor, pulls on shorts, shirt, and trousers, socks and shoes. And then in the bathroom again, tying his tie before the mirror, he says to the pale old man, "That's a nice tie. But *you* don't look too good. All right, never mind. Let's go."

In the upstairs hall, struggling into his jacket, he pauses and listens. He can hear Louisa splashing water in the kitchen. He starts down the staircase, then pauses again. The sound of the water has stopped. He waits. Good—she isn't coming out, she's going to the basement. He goes down to the front door, opens it, and closes it behind him as gently as he can. The outside air is warm, the sun is warm, the smooth tar of the driveway looks soft, like his blanket. He goes around the house to the garage and is relieved to see that the overhead door is up. He has yelled at them a thousand times to put that door down, but now he is glad they always forget. He climbs into the big black car, takes the key from behind the sun visor, switches on the ignition. These Lincolns, bless them—they never fail him. He backs out slowly into the turnaround and heads down the driveway. In the rearview mirror he sees Louisa in the driveway behind him, her mouth stretched wide on a shout, her arms waving. He ignores her and, speeding up, turns into the road toward town.

It is lovely to drive too fast toward his Pleasure Dome through this bright May morning. Lovely to have another opening day. Lovely to have a new ride to christen, the first since the Bumper Cars four years ago. The lake, whizzing by beside him, is studded with bright diamonds of sunlight that flash and wink at him. He feels supremely happy, and then, suddenly, supremely dizzy. No! No blacking out, old man. Not today. Work to do. He turns the rearview mirror so that he can see himself in it, and says to his reflection, "Hold on. Hold on."

Coming into town, he grips the steering wheel tightly, confused by a welter of traffic that has suddenly appeared out of nowhere. Ahead, the cars are pulling off along both sides of the road. The parking lot must be full already. His vision blurs, he blinks, and sees something rushing up at him, a group of people walking in the road. He veers sharply to the right to avoid them and sees, too late, the man getting out of a car, the wide-open door. There is a sickening thump, an explosion of glass, a screech of metal, all mixed together in a whirl. The Lincoln lurches. But keeps going. Herbert clings to the wheel. Can't stop now. Have to get to the park. Must be almost ten.

Somehow he finds his special parking place, rams the Lincoln into it. The swimmy feeling sways just behind his eyes as he slams the car door, but he shoves his way fiercely through a swarm of people at the Pleasure Dome gates. "Hey, buddy, whatcha think yer doin'?" a man complains as Herbert shoulders him aside, but he keeps going, hurrying along the boardwalk through the noise, the music, the smell of popcorn and hot dogs and dust. Shining giant wheels revolve around him, little cars speed by on oily tracks. Two girls, turning upside down in the cage of the Dipsy-Doodle, shriek as he passes them. He pauses for an instant at the merry-go-round as the lions, tawny, glistening, rising and falling side by side, leap toward him, circle by, disappear. He tries to smile at them, but his face feels funny. It doesn't want to do what he asks of it. He goes on, stumbling a little, to the end of the boardwalk, and hears at last a loudspeaker, sees a deep circle of people.

"AND NOW, IN THE ABSENSE OF THE OWNER AND CREATOR OF THE ROWBARGE PLEASURE DOME, MR. HERBERT—"

"I'm here!" he yells. "I'm here!"

The crowd turns, parts, lets him through. Walter is standing at the steps that lead down to the row of pretty boats waiting at the mouth of the Tunnel of Love. The lake water, channeled into this narrow canal, slaps gently at the swan-shaped sides of the boats. Between two posts set into the edge of the boardwalk just above the steps, a wide pink ribbon has been stretched and tied in a fat, romantic bow. Walter pauses, drops the hand that holds the micro-

phone. "Uncle Herbert!" he says in an urgent whisper. "You shouldn't be here! Good Lord, how'd you
get here?"

"I drove," says Herbert. "I'm going to take the first
ride, just like I always do."

"But—"

"Now, listen, Walter, it's still my park. Make the
announcement and let's get on with it."

Walter shrugs. "Well, okay, I guess if you're all
right . . ."

"Of course I'm all right," says Herbert dizzily. His
voice sounds funny to him. Thick.

There is so much noise around them, Walter
doesn't seem to notice. He lifts the microphone.
*"LADIES AND GENTLEMEN, WE'RE IN LUCK
AFTER ALL. THE OWNER AND CREATOR OF
THE ROWBARGE PLEASURE DOME, MR. HER-
BERT ROWBARGE, IS HERE TO CHRISTEN THE
TUNNEL OF LOVE AND TAKE THE FIRST RIDE.
MR. ROWBARGE, IF YOU WILL, PLEASE—CUT
THE RIBBON!"* The loudspeaker over their heads
blares Walter's words out over the park a fraction of
a second after Walter speaks them. Cut-tut the-uh
ribbon-bon.

Herbert reaches for the pair of scissors Walter
holds out to him, but his arm feels funny. "You do
it," he hisses. "Come on. Hurry up."

Walter cuts the ribbon, and the crowd applauds.
Someone in the back whistles. Walter takes Herbert's
arm and guides him down the steps and into the first
boat, settling him on its pink-painted seat. "All right,"

he says in Herbert's ear, "one ride and then I'm taking you home."

A switch is thrown, and Herbert glides forward into the mouth of the tunnel. At intervals, the other little boats come after him, and soon they are all floating, in that dim and watery place, away from the dust and the noise and the people, farther and farther away.

A trooper shoves through the crowd, takes Walter by the shoulder. "Where is he?" he says.

"Who?" says Walter, startled.

"Mr. Rowbarge."

"He's in the tunnel. He's taking the first ride. Why? What's wrong?"

"Accident. Back on Park Street. Mr. Rowbarge run a man down and didn't stop."

"Oh, my God," says Walter. "Are you sure it was Mr. Rowbarge?"

"You bet," says the trooper. "A lot of people seen him. Everyone knows that Lincoln of his. I looked at it out in the parking lot. Right fender's all bashed in."

"The ride only takes a few minutes," says Walter, "so he'll be out pretty soon. Good Lord. How awful. Is the man he hit all right?"

"You kidding? Ambulance is on its way, but he'll never make it to the hospital. Prob'ly dead already. Face all cut up. Lincoln hit him in the back while he was gettin' out of his car. Shoved him through the window of the door."

"Oh, my God. Who was it? Someone from here?"

"No, kid with 'im said they come down from San-dusky for the day. Kid said the old guy's name was Schwimmbeck—Otto Schwimmbeck."

"Never heard the name before."

"No. Pretty bad for the kid. Said he was the old guy's grandson. Maybe twelve or fourteen." The trooper pauses, and then he adds, impressed, "Jeez! Door on that Buick damn near snapped right off."

"Wait," says Walter. "Here come the boats."

The water at the heart-shaped mouth of the Tunnel of Love breaks into bubbles, a low wave rushes forward. And out from that dim and watery place come the little boats, out into the sunlight one by one. In the first boat slumps the figure of the owner and creator, Herbert Rowbarge, the eyes closed, the hands palm-upward on the seat, the face relaxed and blissful.

"Uncle Herbert!" cries Walter.

But Herbert doesn't hear. He has floated deep into the mirror and found his only love, and they are gone.

Thursday, June 5, 1952

Babe and Louisa Rowbarge stand in the hall of their father's house, knee-deep in suitcases, cartons, and shopping bags. Three coats are draped across one suitcase, hangers still caught in the shoulders, and on top of these is a stack of paperback mystery novels tied up with a bathrobe belt, and a tall rubber boot from which the cords of a heating pad and a curling iron twist like living vines.

"Where's the other boot?" Louisa asks.

"I don't know," says Babe. "I couldn't find it anywhere."

Louisa surveys the mess and says, hopelessly, "I had no idea we had so much stuff at Aunt Opal's."

"Well," says Babe, "there was the closet, of course, and the bureau, and all our things in the medicine chest, remember, and then there were the two bookshelves and our pictures, and . . . well, five *years'* worth. That's a long time. You can pile up a lot in five years."

"I guess so," says Louisa. She bends and pokes in the nearest shopping bag, retrieves a book of cross-word puzzles, and flips through the pages.

"There's lots in there that isn't done yet," says Babe defensively.

"Oh, no, Babe, that's all right," says Louisa. "I think you did exactly right, bringing everything. It's just that we'll have to put it all away before supper, because if we don't, Daddy'll . . ." She catches herself and they look at each other and then look away.

"Well!" says Babe. "I'm starving."

"Yes, let's eat," says Louisa. "Fawn made tuna salad and iced tea. She said to tell you she was sorry she couldn't stay to welcome you back, but it got too late."

"I know," says Babe. "I didn't think it would take me so long to pack up."

"It was nice of Walter to lend us his car," says Louisa. "How long can we keep it?"

"He wants it back tomorrow afternoon," says Babe. "So we'll have to decide what to do."

"I guess so," says Louisa.

They wade away from the mess and soon they are eating at the dining-room table. Louisa has lit the candles and Babe has poured them each a little glass of wine. They are stiff with each other, and uncomfortable, and talk very little at first, but soon the wine begins to warm them and Louisa puts down her fork. "Babe," she begins, "I don't know how to say this, but . . . well, the thing is . . ."

"I know," says Babe. "You don't feel anything. Neither do I."

"What's the matter with us?"

"There's nothing the matter with us," says Babe. "Probably it just hasn't sunk in yet."

"Actually," says Louisa, "I do feel something. What I feel is I'm really upset because I don't feel anything."

"I know," says Babe. "It's all right. Don't worry."

"I thought the house would feel empty. You know? But it just feels like it has more . . . *air* in it somehow."

Babe looks around with a frown. "Maybe we should redecorate," she says. "Throw everything out and start from scratch."

"You mean curtains? And chairs and . . . *carpets*?" Louisa asks, amazed.

"Well, yes. If we're going to do it at all," says Babe, "we should do it right down to the bath mats."

"That would cost a lot," says Louisa. "But still, I guess we can afford it. It's queer, though, isn't it, Daddy's leaving half his money to us and the other half to Walter. You'd think he'd have divided it in thirds."

"I think he more or less forgot there were two of us," says Babe. "But I don't care, do you? It's still a lot of money."

"A whole lot," says Louisa. "What in the world will we do with it all?"

"I don't know," says Babe.

"We could go to blues and whites," suggests Louisa. "When we do the house over. With little touches of pink."

"And yellow," Babe agrees. "Yellow makes a nice accent."

Warming to the project now, Louisa says, "Do you think we could get a television set? Everybody's got them now, and we're probably missing a lot."

"You're right," says Babe. "We should get a television set. Maybe even two. One for the living room, and another one upstairs. In our bedroom."

"Two!" Louisa exclaims.

"Well, we *could*," says Babe. "If we *want* to."

They gaze at each other in wonder. Babe gets up, brings the bottle of wine to the table, and fills up their glasses. "And then there's the matter of the car," she says, sitting down again. "Daddy's is just too . . . well, I suppose we could get it repaired, but . . ."

"Oh, no," says Louisa with a shudder. "That would be gruesome. I could never drive it again."

"Me, either," says Babe with relief. "So *that's* settled."

Louisa brightens. "I wonder if we're too old for a convertible."

"We're not too old for anything," says Babe firmly. "A convertible would be just the ticket. In case we want to go to Florida."

"Florida!"

"Well, Walter said we ought to go down to Florida. Sarasota, maybe. Get away for a rest to somewhere with a nice beach."

"That's an awfully long drive," says Louisa.

"But Walter said we wouldn't have to drive," Babe explains. "He said we could fly, and have the car shipped down on the train."

"But, Babe, we've never even *been* in an airplane."

"Everybody does it now, though, I guess," says Babe.

"Well, I suppose if we're having the house redone, they could put in the carpeting while we're gone," says Louisa. "So I wouldn't have to see it rolled up."

"That's right," says Babe. "It could all be done by the time we got back."

They are silent, then, eyes round, thinking. After a while Louisa says, "It was a nice funeral."

"Yes," says Babe, "it really was. Nicer than Uncle Stuart's, with the weather so warm and all. And Dr. Bray gave a wonderful eulogy, didn't you think so?"

"Yes," says Louisa, "but that was hard. To listen to, I mean."

"Well, we'll never have to do it again," says Babe.

After a moment Louisa says, carefully, "Babe, we probably won't want to throw *everything* out. I . . . I'm sort of fond of the living room the way it is."

"Well, I am, too, actually," says Babe. "And the curtains are practically new."

"And this is a nice room," says Louisa, looking around.

"Yes, it really is. Daddy had good taste. I've always liked this wallpaper."

They look at each other. There is a long pause, and then Babe says, "Of course, if we don't want to go as far as Florida, there's some really nice beaches right up on Lake Erie."

"That's so," says Louisa eagerly. "Why, there must be plenty of places with good hotels and everything."

"I'm sure of it," says Babe. "If we did that, we wouldn't have to ship the car at all. We could just drive up and back."

"That's better, anyway," says Louisa. "That way, you're not tied down to airplane reservations. Why did Walter think we ought to go to Florida?"

"I don't know," says Babe. "He just said it would be good for us. But after that," she goes on, hesitantly, "Aunt Opal said we ought to go to *Europe* in the fall. She said she'd go with us." She pauses. "Louisa, do you want to go to Europe?"

Louisa takes a sip of wine and sets her glass down carefully. At last she says, in a small voice, "Well, not a whole lot."

"But neither do I!" cries Babe, clapping her hands together. "Not at *all*!"

They look at each other again, and all at once they begin to laugh. "I don't even want to go to Lake *Erie*!" Louisa manages.

"Nope," Babe whoops, "not in the least. And I'll tell you something else. I don't want to redecorate our bedroom. I *love* our bedroom. I think it's beautiful!"

"We'd look pretty silly in a convertible, as far as that goes," says Louisa, wiping her eyes.

Babe pushes back her plate. "Louisa," she says, "we don't have to do what Walter says. Or Aunt Opal, either. From now on, we can do what *we* want."

"I guess they'll think we're pretty dull," says Louisa.

"Well, so what?" says Babe. "Might as well face it. We *are* dull. Old and plain and dull."

"But rich," says Louisa. "Don't forget that. Old, plain, dull, and *rich*."

Babe stands up. "What time is it?" she asks.

"It's . . . let's see . . . it's so dark in here . . . it's eight-thirty," says Louisa, peering at her watch.

"Perfect," says Babe. "There's just time. For the second show. If we hurry."

"Oh, Babe, *lovely*. What's playing?"

"*I* don't know," says Babe. "What difference does it make?"

"None!" cries Louisa. "It doesn't matter in the least."

"And afterwards," says Babe, "we'll go to the Frostee-Freeze and get a hot-fudge sundae."

"With nuts," says Louisa, "and a cherry."

Babe nods. "Nuts, and a cherry, and a great big gob of whipped cream."

But before they go out to Walter's car, waiting in the warm June night that hangs so full of stars and peepers and the far-off music of the Pleasure Dome, they carry their dishes to the kitchen, put away the wine, and carefully blow out the candles. Then they go, each, to a separate bathroom, and behind the two closed doors, with the water running, they each give in, quietly, to a backed-up rush of tears, trying, with tissues pressed against their eyes, not to name the reason. Afterward, they splash their faces with cold water and, meeting again in the hall, they leave the house, locking the door behind them, and drive away, with Babe at the wheel, together.